"I love *The Ornament Keeper*. For such a little Christmas book, it packs a big literary wallop for everyday life. It is a strong, powerful, raw story with a deeply moving message of forgiveness that I believe will literally save marriages. Don't miss it!"

—Brian Bird, screenwriter and executive producer, *When Calls the Heart* and *The Case for Christ*

"A warm and hope-filled novella that sparkles like the shining ornaments on a Christmas tree. Everson tells the story of a marriage gone astray and a woman wrestling with how to get it back. As Felicia unwraps precious ornaments from the past, the reader glimpses the couple's first taste of love, the choice from yesteryear that threatens to ruin them, and the meandering path that forgiveness sometimes takes. A sweet and thought-provoking Christmas read."

—Elizabeth Musser, Christy Award finalist and author of *The Long Highway Home, The Swan House,* and *The Sweetest Thing*

"In *The Ornament Keeper*, Eva Marie Everson reminds readers that sometimes our biggest problems live inside our own hearts and heads. And what better time to find healing than Christmas? Everson offers a deeply relatable story with her trademark Southern style. Snuggle in, bring a tissue, and prepare to do a little soul searching of your own."

—Sarah Loudin Thomas, award-winning author *The Sound of Rain, Miracle in a Dry Season,* and *Until the Harvest*

"With delightful charm and uncanny insight, Eva Marie Everson takes the premise of a shotgun wedding and fast forwards to its roiling repercussions, nearly twenty years and three children later. Everson ca~~ptivates the reader in a story of th~~ ____ l taken with the best intenti____ ____mes of miscom- munication ____ *The Ornament Keeper* spe____ ng which of our so-called p____ ted. Against the

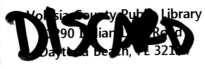

backdrop of a day-in-and-day-out marriage, this engaging parable looks at a life assembled through attention to the little things. The path to its satisfying conclusion is an enjoyable saunter, its traces the kind that linger for weeks."

—Claire Fullerton, author of *Mourning Dove*

"Everson's *The Ornament Keeper* is a beautiful example of a common belief in psychology: we're only as sick as our secrets. Even—as in this book—when the secret is not kept from others, but hidden within the self. *The Ornament Keeper* played out inside my clinic over and over again. Everson shows brilliant insight into anxiety disorders."

—Merilyn Howton Marriott, LPCS, and author of
The Children of Main Street

"Leesha and Jackson's story moved me to empathy, frustration, and ultimately tears of gratitude. With honesty and humor, Eva Marie Everson expertly reveals the secrets of a wife trying to uncover the roots of her discontentment. I saw myself in Leesha, and I hurt for her, myself, and women like us who carry unresolved burdens, especially those burdens we don't readily see in ourselves. *The Ornament Keeper* is a beautiful testimony of God's faithfulness to work in us, even when we don't recognize His hand."

—Shellie Arnold, author of *The Spindle Chair, Sticks and Stones,* and *Abide With Me,* and founder of YOUR MARRIAGE resources

The
ORNAMENT
KEEPER

A CHRISTMAS NOVELLA

EVA MARIE EVERSON

NEW HOPE®
PUBLISHERS

An imprint of Iron Stream Media
Birmingham, Alabama

New Hope® Publishers
5184 Caldwell Mill Rd.
St. 204-221
Hoover, AL 35244
NewHopePublishers.com

Library of Congress Cataloging-in-Publication Data

Names: Everson, Eva Marie, author.
Title: The ornament keeper : a Christmas novella / Eva Marie Everson.
Description: Birmingham, Alabama : New Hope Publishers, [2018]
Identifiers: LCCN 2018017785| ISBN 9781563090899 (Permabind) | ISBN 9781563091247 (Ebook)
Subjects: LCSH: Marriage—Fiction. | GSAFD: Christian fiction. | Love stories.
Classification: LCC PS3605.V47 O76 2018 | DDC 813/.6—dc23
LC record available at https://lccn.loc.gov/2018017785

ISBN-13: 978-1-56309-089-9

1 2 3 4 5—22 21 20 19 18

To

Sandra D. Bricker

1958–2016

I will never forget you.

I will always miss you.

~Merry Christmas~

A Few of the Novels by Eva Marie Everson

The One True Love of Alice-Ann

God Bless Us Every One

Five Brides

The Road to Testament

Unconditional

This Fine Life

Things Left Unspoken

The Cedar Key Novels

Chasing Sunsets

Waiting for Sunrise

Slow Moon Rising

The Potluck Club Novels

(coauthor with Linda Evans Shepherd)

The Potluck Club

The Potluck Club: Trouble's Brewing

The Potluck Club Takes the Cake

The Secret's in the Sauce

Bake Until Golden

A Taste of Fame

A Few of Eva Marie Everson's Nonfiction Books

The Final Race: The Incredible World War II Story of the Olympian Who Inspired Chariots of Fire (coauthor with Eric T. Eichinger)

The Bipolar Experience (coauthor with LeeAnn Jefferies)

The Potluck Club Cookbook (coauthor with Linda Evans Shepherd)

Reflections of God's Holy Land (coauthor with Miriam Feinberg Vamosh)

Common Mistakes Writers Make

Sex, Lies, and the Media (coauthor with Jessica Everson)

Sex, Lies, and High School (coauthor with Jessica Everson)

Oasis

CHAPTER ONE

Christmas Season 2018

I pushed the Keurig lever down on a decaf dark roast pod. "I've made a decision," I said, hoping my voice sounded as sure as I wanted it to. Because I had. More or less. Sort of.

"What's that?" Sara, my nineteen-year-old daughter, sat at the table behind me.

The coffeemaker sighed, telling me that eight ounces of water had been poured over ground coffee beans and now waited in the mug. I lifted the lever, removed the pod, lowered the lever, and pushed buttons for an additional four ounces of water to weaken the drink I found too strong for my taste. As it brewed, I added a teaspoon of sugar and then reached for the half-n-half Sara had left on the counter. I unscrewed the cap, sniffed the carton, and waited for the water to stop dripping.

"Mom?"

I glanced over my shoulder. "Oh. Yes. Just a sec." I poured creamer into the coffee and stirred, making a bigger to-do out of it than necessary. Even for me.

"I've decided," I said, joining Sara, who hunched over a bowl of Cheerios, "to not put any Christmas decorations out this year." I opened my eyes wide, daring her to object.

Her gaze met mine as a drop of milk escaped between her lips. She swallowed, wiped her mouth with a napkin she kept wadded in her left hand, and said, "Say that again."

My coffee mug clunked on the old farmhouse table I'd restored when we'd purchased the rambling four-bedroom Victorian—the one with the mother-in-law suite located down a short hall from the kitchen.

Just in case.

"Swallow, Sara."

Her head came up fully, thick blond tresses spilling over her shoulder as she did. California-sky blue eyes blinked at me in disbelief. "Because of Dad?"

I brought the coffee mug to my lips, blew, and took a tentative swallow while my eyes managed to find and travel along one of the scars within the table's wood. "Yes."

Sara picked up her nearly finished bowl of cereal and walked to the sink to rinse it and place it in the dishwasher. I studied her—the height of her—which she inherited from her father—the jutting hip bones—which she'd gotten from me—and the way her pajama bottoms barely hung on to them.

Fluffy sheep jumping over bright yellow stars.

I blinked, looking up as she turned toward me and leaned against the counter. She pushed the sleeves of a university tee to her elbows as though she'd suddenly grown hot, then brought the ball of one bare foot to rest against the top of the other. "So what you're saying is that because Dad's no longer with us, we're not going to celebrate this family's most important holiday."

I leaned into the hard back of the spindle chair. "I just don't have the energy this year, Sara." Couldn't she see that? Couldn't my wise, oldest child take one look at me and see how difficult the past four months had been?

Sara threw up her hands as though in defeat. Strange, because we really hadn't had the humdinger of a fight I'd expected. "Well, that's just peachy, Mom. I guess without Dad here, Travis and Hank and I mean nothing to you."

My brow furrowed. "Don't even *think* that."

She leaned against the countertop, arms crossed, thick pink lips pursed. Another feature she'd gotten from her father. I raked my teeth across my own to keep from thinking about Jackson's. The way they felt when he'd kissed me. Especially that first time . . . and the last.

If I could remember it.

"Sara, between keeping the house and going to work and—and just dealing with your father not being here . . . I'm tired, sweetheart, and I don't—I don't know if I have the energy this year to—to go get the tree. To cut it down. To get it home. To string the lights. To . . ." I couldn't finish.

Sara crossed the room, taking the chair next to mine and wrapping me in an awkward but tight hug. "Mom. I know. I do." She squeezed as she whispered words of encouragement, then sat back, taking my hands in hers, long fingers entwining. "Look. I know this year will be hard. The hardest. But . . . but, look. I've got my own truck, you know."

Yes, I knew. Again, so much like her father. Why buy a car when Ram made trucks? he'd always say . . .

"Travis and Hank and I can go to Steadman's Christmas Tree Farm. We can cut the tree. We can haul it home, and Travis and I will even get the lights up."

I stared at our hands, still laced together at their fingers. "But, Sara . . . the ornaments."

"Mom," she said. "Look at me."

I did. When had she grown into such a woman? When had she become my heart's protector?

"Mom. I'll help you. The boys and I both will." She grinned. "And let's see if Washburn's is selling tinsel this year. Let's make it the most traditional tree it can be."

I attempted to smile. "I don't think department stores have sold that stuff in years."

"Then I'll order it off Amazon." She grinned at me. "You know they're not just about selling books, right? They sell everything from books to bras."

My shoulders sagged as I tried not to laugh. "Sara . . ."

"Mom. Come on. If not for yourself and if not for me . . . for the boys. Especially little Hank. Won't this year be hard enough on him?"

She had a point. "All right," I conceded. "But make sure the tree is a good one."

Sara released my hands and gave the world a fist-pump.

"A Fraser. Fat and tall. Not thin and squatty."

"I know, I know." She stood, pulled her sleeves back to her wrists. The bands had stretched, and I frowned. That tee had cost nearly thirty outlandish dollars. "And stop looking at the bands of my sleeves," she ordered. "They'll go back as soon as you wash them."

I gave her a half-smile. "Will they?" I asked. Did anything ever really "go back" after it had been stretched out of shape?

She planted a kiss on top of my head. "They will. Promise." Sara started out of the kitchen. "I gotta go get ready for work."

"When will you get the tree?" I asked, now feeling ready to get the whole ordeal over with.

"After work. I'll come get the boys and we'll go."

A half hour later I took the final sip of tepid coffee as Sara returned to the kitchen. She wore a pair of skinny jeans and hooded sweatshirt over her work tee. The one that advertised Morgan's Auto Parts Store. *The Champion of Auto Parts . . .*

Jackson's store. No, Jackson's *life.*

"Are the boys still asleep?" I asked.

"I can only assume. I haven't heard a peep out of either of them." She opened the pantry door and pulled a packet of cheese and peanut butter crackers from its box. Her go-to snack. "Tell them I'll pick them up around five thirty."

I nodded.

Sara squeezed my shoulder. I looked up at her and smiled. "You smell good," I said.

"It's a Vince Camuto," she said. "A little girlier than I usually go for, but . . . Billy got it for me."

Billy. The boy she'd dated since they'd met each other at college. They'd been infatuated with each other, really. Which worried me all the more. And made me glad she still came home on weekends to work in the store. "Well, it smells nice."

"Thanks. You gonna be okay?"

I nodded. "I've got a lot of laundry to catch up on. Some bills to pay."

Sara pulled her iPhone from her back pocket and checked the time. "I gotta go. You know how the boss man gets if I'm late."

Did I ever . . . "Okay."

"Anything you want me to tell him?" she asked from the door leading to the garage. Her voice sounded hopeful. The expression on her face, expectant.

"Uh—tell him—tell him I said—tell him I said I hope he has a nice Saturday."

Her face fell. "Good one, Mom." She opened the door, swept through, and closed it behind her.

"What was I supposed to say?" I asked the air around me. "Merry Christmas?"

CHAPTER TWO

After dinner, while my children drove to the Christmas tree farm to find the perfect tree, I gave the kitchen a quick cleaning, then went into the guest bedroom, opened the walk-in closet, and stared down the red and green bins holding all the seasonal paraphernalia. "Well," I said to them, "here we are again."

I placed my hands on my hips, unsure as to where to begin. I'd agreed to the tree—to the lights and the ornaments—but what about the crèche? What about the faux evergreen boughs I so carefully placed along the fireplace mantels? The candles? The Mark Roberts holiday figurines?

I reached for the bin holding the nativity set, brought it out into the bedroom, knelt before it, and opened the top. Mary stared up at me through the haze of bubble wrap, and I sighed, remembering.

"Look at her," I'd said to my husband when I'd spied her in the antique market. "Isn't she something?"

❄

Christmas Season, 1999

Jackson ambled up beside me, his thickly muscled arms laden with plastic bags of this and that we'd already purchased.

"Leesha," he said. "Do we *need* this?"

"Oh, Jackson," I breathed out, my fingertips lightly touching her delicate features. "And look at how sweet the baby Jesus is laying there."

Jackson nudged me. "And there's poor Joseph leaning on his staff," he teased. "Poor man doesn't have a clue what's hit him."

I frowned up at my six-foot-six husband of nearly one year. "Very funny, Jackson Morgan. And completely sacrilegious. I'm sure he knew."

"I'm sure he didn't." Jackson raised his arms, the plastic bags coming with them. "Now, listen. You've spent all we can afford to spend right now on these *old* bowls," he said. "And why, I'll never know."

I pouted, hoping to get my way with him. If I'd learned one thing in our brief marriage, it was how to get my way. "They're not *old*. They're antiques. And think how pretty they'll look on our cute little table on Christmas day when we have your mom and my dad over." I linked my arm with his and squeezed. "Besides, you can't get new stuff like this."

"None of it matches," he said, his brow furrowed.

I kissed his shoulder, then nibbled at it. "It's called eclectic."

Jackson bent down to give me a kiss. "That's called dirty pool."

"Does that mean I can have the nativity set?"

He kissed me again. "No. It means we can't afford it, no matter how cute you try to be."

I let out a deep sigh, and stroked the top of the stable. Jackson was right. Our budget *was* limited, more than I'd ever dream of before Sara was born. I walked away.

But the crèche found its way under the tree that year, along with the annual ornament nestled in the toe of my stocking.

❄

Christmas Season 2018

"Oh, Jackson," I whispered past the knot in my chest and in the silence of the guest room as I unwrapped the mother of our Lord. "How you surprised me."

I took a deep breath and went back to work. By the time the children returned, red-cheeked and singing carols off-key, I had managed to pull all the Christmas stuff into the living room. I stood at the stove, stirring hot cocoa when the front door opened and the first shouts of glee entered the warmth inside. "Mom," my second born called. "Come look!"

I turned the burner off before hurrying to the front of the house. Travis, fourteen and looking more like his father than his father at the same age, clapped his hands as he hustled toward me. "Wait till you see."

Seven-year-old Hank dashed behind his brother. "Mom," he said. "Santa's gonna freak *out* when he sees this tree."

I laughed as he ran into my arms and I lifted him. The release of positive emotion felt good. Freeing. As though the past few months had never happened. That I'd not lived through their nightmare. *Our* nightmare. "You think?" I asked, nuzzling his neck, wondering how much longer I'd be able to hold him this way.

"I *know*," he shouted, throwing his head back.

I ruffled his hair—dark, like mine. The only child who had somehow managed to let my genes define his appearance. "Well, let's see this tree."

Travis returned to the double front doors, opened them both wide, and then hurried out to the truck backed into the semicircular driveway. I walked out behind him, Hank still on my hip, and felt the blast of December air hit me straight on. "Brrr," I said, burying my nose into Hank's neck. "You didn't get too cold out at the farm, did you?"

"No, Mom," he said, placing his hands on both sides of my face. "Sissy made me keep my jacket on."

I drew him closer. "Good, because I couldn't have you getting sick before Santa comes."

"Mom," Travis hollered from the back of the truck where a thick evergreen lay in the bed, its silvery branches shimmering in the moonlight. "See? We did good. It's a Fraser."

"Your favorite," Sara called.

"I love the scent," I said, unsure if I'd spoken loud enough to be heard.

But even as I said the words, Jackson's voice crossed through the years.

❄

December 23, 1998

We stood in my pastor's living room. Young. Our futures in front of us. Behind us. We were scared. Terrified really. Jackson's mother dabbed at her eyes with a lavender handkerchief. The old-fashioned, linen kind. My father remained ramrod straight next to Brother Evan and Miss Arlene's Christmas tree, which stood in the center of a bay window. Unable to look at Jackson's mother, too crushed to look at my father, and too shy to peer up at Jackson's face, I kept my focus instead on the tree. And on what looked to be a thousand lights and ornaments.

Jackson leaned over to whisper, "I like the way that tree smells." The warmth of his breath sent shivers down my arms and I crossed them, rubbing them with my hands.

"I like the way the branches are green on the top and silver on the bottom."

Miss Arlene—blonde, coiffed, and vivacious—entered the room from the kitchen. "It's a Fraser fir," she said, beaming at us. She kissed my cheek. "I've prepared some little cupcakes with bridal white icing and some punch for after the ceremony."

Tears blurred my vision. "Thank you, Miss Arlene."

"Well," Brother Evan said, his footsteps echoing on the wood floor as he walked in from the foyer. He held up a small black book. "I've got my lines. Y'all know yours?"

Jackson chuckled as he took my trembling hand in his thick one.

This was it.

"Ready, Champ?" Brother Evan asked, using the same endearment Jackson's father had always called him.

"Yes, sir," Jackson said, his voice croaking.

"Felicia?" he asked me, a little more tender.

I took a deep breath, unable to answer, and allowed the sweet scent of the holiday tree to fill me.

❄

Christmas Season 2018

Sara and Travis hauled the tree out of the truck, up the front porch steps, and through the open double doors. Hank and I hurried in after them. I put my youngest on the floor so he could run behind his older siblings and then quickly closed the front doors, locking them. I shivered, mostly from the cold. Partly from the memory.

Had Jackson been there, he would have fussed about the electricity. About my having left the doors open. But I couldn't dwell on that right now.

"Where's the stand?" Travis asked as I rounded into the wide living room where a fire crackled in the white marble fireplace.

I pointed to the bin nearest the front window. A bay, just like Brother Evan and Miss Arlene's. "Right there."

Sara dug into it while Travis righted the tree. "What do you say, Mom?"

I pressed my hands together as if in prayer. "It's perfect," I said. And it very nearly was.

CHAPTER THREE

"Okay, treesome-threesome," I teased once the lights had been strung, plugged in for testing, and the dead bulbs replaced. "It is time for all God's children to go upstairs and get ready for bed."

I gathered up the empty mugs of cocoa as they pretended that my declaration had been a sentence worse than a trip to a dental office, something none of my kids were overly fond of. "Now, now. You all knew we wouldn't be trimming the tree tonight."

Hank jumped up and down, the lights from the tree shimmering in his dark-brown eyes. "Mommy, what will we do tomorrow?"

I squatted in front of him. "Tomorrow we hang the door wreaths." I looked up at Sara. "Did you get wreaths? I forgot to remind you."

She smiled in understanding. "I got them. They're still in the back of the truck."

Standing, I looked at Travis who replaced a bin lid. "Sweetheart, run outside and get them. It's supposed to get awful cold tonight."

He looked at me, a giant question mark forming over his head. "They're *plants,* Mom. They're going to be outside for the rest of the month anyhow."

I cocked an eyebrow to show him I meant business.

"Yeah, yeah," he said before heading back outside.

Sara reached for Hank's hand. "Come on, squirt. Time for you to get upstairs." She led him to the oak staircase with its ornate balustrade and original stained-glass windows running alongside it and guided him upward before coming back to me. "Mom," she said gently. "Do you want me to put *the* ornaments on? I can do it before I head back to Southern tomorrow afternoon."

I shook my head. "No. That's my job. At least the first ones—the ones from your father—as always."

"I know, but—I thought—this year . . ."

I looked at the bin housing the ornaments. All of them special. Some handmade by my children and given with pride on Christmas morning. Many of them expensive works of art. And a few of them—nineteen to be exact—priceless beyond measure. "No," I repeated. "That's my job."

✳

Christmas Season, 1998

After our makeshift, private wedding at Brother Evan and Miss Arlene's, Jackson carried me over the threshold of the studio apartment my father had paid first and last months' rent for and Mrs. Morgan had covered the utility deposits for. For two people old enough to get pregnant, we sure hadn't readied ourselves financially.

Once inside, Jackson set my feet back on the floor, then turned to flip on the light switch. In many ways, I wished he would leave it off. I felt strangely shy in front of the man I'd made a baby with but had never *really* known intimately. "Home sweet home," he said as he closed the door.

The space felt foreign, even though we'd spent the past week decorating it, turning it from a cold, empty cave to something warm and inviting. Goodwill-purchased kitchen items, a used sofa, end table and lamp we'd bought at a garage sale. A kitchenette table and two chairs Jackson had found on the side of the road sat beneath the one window in the entire room. "All it needs is a coat of paint," he'd said, beaming at his find.

So I painted it white and covered it in a linen tablecloth that had once belonged to my mother, hoping to add a homey feel to the room.

The only thing new in the entire four-hundred-and-sixty-five square feet was a basic mattress and box springs set along with some new linens, all which Jackson had purchased with his savings because, "Do you know how hard it is to find a bed for a six-foot-six man?"

I admitted, then, that I didn't. Now, newly married to the man, I still didn't. Not yet, anyway.

"Do you want to use the bathroom first or anything?" he asked, dropping his keys on the end table.

Heat rushed to my face. "Sure," I said. My best friend Callie and I had brought my clothes over earlier that day. My toiletries and a few other personal items. By the time we got there, Jackson had already hung his clothes on one half of the narrow walk-in closet, taking up twice as much space as most men.

Jackson loved his clothes.

I went into the closet and opened the chest of drawers at the far end where I'd neatly put my underwear, pulled out a pair, then opened another drawer where I'd placed several pairs of pajamas. I reached for the ones on top. Flannel, baggy bottoms. Long-sleeved button-up top. Fuzzy socks to keep my feet warm. Not exactly what I'd always imagined I'd wear on my wedding night.

After a hot shower and brushing my teeth and my hair—which I pulled into a haphazard half-bun, half-ponytail—I returned to the main part of the studio. Jackson sat relaxed on the sofa, watching *It's a Wonderful Life*.

"My mother loved that movie," I said, partially for lack of anything better to say. Partially because it was true.

He looked at me, and his eyes widened. I supposed he'd expected me in something different than flannel too. Then, just as quickly, his expression softened and he said, "Your mother was nothing short of a classic herself."

He had that much right.

My eyes flickered to the bed in the far corner, kept separate from the living area by a latticework divider that had been in my college dorm room. If I'd ever experienced a more awkward moment in my life, I couldn't remember it.

Jackson scooted up on the sofa, stretched his arms, and said, "Look here. Why don't you go ahead and get some sleep? You must be exhausted."

Which meant what? That he'd join me right away? Or would he keep watching the movie? Find out if a bell ringing really meant an angel earned its wings?

"What about you?" I asked, still standing in the same spot I'd seemed riveted to the last five minutes.

He glanced down the tiny hallway. "I'm going to shower in a bit." His blue eyes peered up at me through wheat-blond errant bangs. "Look, Leesha. You can relax. This is weird for both of us, but probably more you than me. I'm smart enough to realize that."

I clasped my hands together in front of me. "I'm sorry—"

He shook his head. "No. Don't be. I'm the one—I'm the one who messed things up. You and I had a rock-solid friendship, and I'm the one who took things too far."

I sat on the sofa as far from him as possible without falling off the edge. "Jackson, it's not like you forced—"

"I was just so—so—"

"Sad."

"—that night. Losing my dad—"

"I understand losing a parent."

"—that way." He paused, allowed the conversation to catch up to itself. "I know you do." He rested his elbows on his knees. Laced his fingers together. Stared down at his feet, still wearing dress shoes. "I just want you to know . . . I'm going to try—" His eyes found mine again. "With everything I've got to make this right for you. Whatever you need. Whatever it takes."

I smiled, unsure how to respond. "And I'll do my best too. For you."

Just not that *night.*

He sighed, his broad shoulders curving under the weight now resting there. "We don't even have a tree," he said. "What kind of a first Christmas will this be without a tree in our new home?"

I'd hardly thought of the studio as our *home*—not yet, anyway—and I'd certainly not worried about it not having a tree. But apparently, Jackson had. "Don't worry," I said. "Tomorrow evening we'll be at your mom's for Christmas Eve. And your brother and sister and their families will be there, and my dad and . . . your mom always has a lovely tree." Which was about all I could say about Jackson's mother right then. The way Mrs. Morgan had looked at me when we'd told her about the baby—as if we'd made our mistake to add to her misery—would stay with me forever.

Jackson said nothing.

"I'm going to bed," I said. "You're right. I'm tired." I stood, wondering if I should give him a goodnight kiss. And if I did, if he would misinterpret it. "Well," I stammered. "Goodnight."

He presented a brave half-smile. "Night, Leesh."

The next day, I entered my new mother-in-law's house the way I always had—with a touch of envy. Jackson's mother's home—despite it being the first Christmas without her husband—looked like a *Southern*

Living magazine Christmas cover. As usual, my eyes drank in the décor . . . the holly, the garland, the crèche, the flickering cinnamon-scented candles. And the tree . . . Gracious, the tree dominated the living room—a room so large our entire studio could fit in it—its branches nearly bowing under the weight of ornaments and lights. Silver- and gold-foiled gifts spread wide along the floor beneath it.

But what caught my eye was the new stocking at the fireplace. The one hanging next to Jackson's. The one with my name on it. My fingertips touched my lips, which had formed a silent "O."

Jackson came up behind me, draped one arm over my shoulder, and whispered, "Didn't see that one coming, did you?"

I smiled up at him. "Did your mother—?"

He blushed. "No."

Of course not. Her graciousness could only go so far. "Then—?"

"If you look closely," he said, "You'll see there's a little something there in the toe."

I turned to him. "Santa's been here already?" I asked, now realizing he'd been the culprit.

"Appears so," he teased. "Go look."

I started to do just that, then stopped. "But, Jackson . . . I didn't get you anything."

His brow shot up. "What? You think *I* put something in that stocking? I believe you were right when you said Santa."

I reached into the velvety depths of it, my fingers curving around something cool to the touch. When I'd brought my hand out, it held a store-bought cookie-dough ornament depicting two Christmas mice. A mister and a missus. Decked out in red, both wearing Santa caps and snuggled under a blanket of red and green. A sweet kiss connected them while, beneath their embrace, the words "Our First Christmas" glimmered in silver. "Oh, Jackson," I said.

"It's not much," he admitted. "The booster club was selling them uptown. I think they ordered them in bulk."

"I don't care," I said. "This means everything."

"Really?"

"Absolutely everything," I said, pressing it against my heart. And I meant it.

Chapter Four

2018

After Jackson and I separated, our children continued to attend the church they'd grown up in. The one Jackson had attended since birth. But sometime during that summer I returned to the church of my childhood. The one my father attended, even after my mother's death. Somehow, he said, being there brought comfort to him, feeling her sitting beside him in the pew as though she really were.

The Sunday after Jackson left our home and our marriage—the one that had come months earlier as August's heat made a final show before the cool of autumn entered—I had walked down the center aisle of Bakersville First Baptist and stepped into the empty spot next to my father. He looked at me, I looked at him, and then we both turned our attention to the pastor without another word. Only after the service ended did Dad peer down at the bulletin he held in both hands, fold it in two, and say, "I reckon the kids are at First Methodist."

"They are," I said. "Sara drove them."

Dad folded the bulletin again, then slipped it into his inside coat pocket. "You think that's best?"

I stared at my father, who had a Richard-Gere-in-his-sixties look about him, and wondered, ridiculously, why the seat beside him remained unoccupied. Why he'd never remarried. He'd never even dated after Mom "left us," as he always put it.

He was certainly handsome and charismatic enough. He'd been romantic to a fault with Mom and generous and loving to his grandchildren and me. As the town's only veterinarian, he made a good living. He would have been a perfect catch for any of the single women in town . . . with the exception of one. Jackson and I used to lie in bed at night and cackle about the possibility of my father and his mother "getting together."

"Oh, heavens, no," I'd say, my hand pressing against my stomach to keep from hurting myself from laughter. "Anything but that . . ."

"Just too weird," Jackson said. *"Our kids with one set of grandparents . . ."*

"The Southern family tree that doesn't fork . . ."

Dad looked at me now, the ice blue of his eyes from behind wire-rimmed glasses meeting mine. "Do you?"

I gripped the gold leaf-paged Bible. "I told them it was their choice." And I had. Even Hank hadn't wanted to come with me to my childhood place of worship.

Dad nodded. "I reckon you gotta do what you see as best for them."

I placed my hand over his and squeezed. "But you don't agree with my decision?"

He stood and I stood with him, happy to note that most of the church members—including the pastor and his wife—had made it back up the aisle and out the double front doors. The last thing I needed was words of commiseration. "Doesn't matter what I think," Dad said while indicating I should find my way into the aisle.

"It matters to me," I said.

Dad smiled. "No, hon. I've never interfered before and I'm not about to start now." He placed his hand on the small of my back and guided me to walk on ahead. "What are your plans for lunch?"

I told him I had none.

"Kids going to be gone most of the day, you think?" he asked.

"I'm expecting they'll go over to Mrs. Morgan's after church."

"Then why don't you and I go out for a bite?" he asked.

And, for the past four months, we'd kept up the show. Every Sunday the boys and Sara (when she was home) went to the church Jackson and I had raised them in, and I met Dad at First Baptist followed by lunch at Steely Joe's Café.

On the Sunday after the children brought the tree home, and during our ritual lunch, I shared with Dad my concern over whether readying the house for Christmas was a good idea or not.

"Why wouldn't it be?" he asked.

I stabbed at fried okra piled high in a small bowl next to a plate of chicken and dumplings—Sunday being the one day I threw my diet to the wind. I'd somehow managed—even after giving birth to three children and the last one being "later in life"—to stay close to the same weight as when Jackson and I married. Giving myself one day to eat as I pleased kept me from binging and putting on more of the middle-age spread than giving birth to three children had caused.

"I don't know, Dad," I said. "I don't want them to get too hopeful . . ."

Dad bit into a fat, glistening fried chicken thigh, chewed, and swallowed. "Too hopeful? About what?"

I rested my fork on the edge of the plate and shook my head. "I don't know. A Christmas miracle maybe?"

"Are you planning on putting out more than the tree?" Dad asked, ignoring my quip.

"I wasn't," I said with a smile. "But then I saw all those decorations . . . the nativity set . . . Mary."

Dad laughed as he wiped his mouth with a paper napkin. "Goodness, I'll never forget that Christmas. The way Jackson surprised you with it."

Oh, yes. Jackson had put his foot down firmly in the antique mart, saying "*absolutely* not," even as I begged and pouted prettily for it. He wasn't spending that much money—money we didn't have, he said, on something we'd only look at a few days a year.

He dealt with my sulking all the way home. The cold supper I prepared later and the cold shoulder I gave him that night when he reached for me beneath the covers. And all the while, unbeknownst to me, he'd called my father while I slapped mayo on bread and asked him to swing by the mart on his way home from work and purchase the crèche. "I'll bring you the money tomorrow," he told him.

And then he did.

That Christmas Day in 1999, as we unwrapped the gifts from under the tree at Dad's, Jackson made me save the "big one for last," then watched my face light up brighter than the eastern star as I realized what the crinkled sheets of newspaper protected within the box. "Oh, Jackson," I said, throwing myself into his arms and kissing him more amorously than I usually did, which seemed to both thrill and shock him. "I can't believe you did this. I really can't believe it."

The nativity set hadn't been his only gift that year. There'd been two others—the first, our daughter Sara, who slept bundled in her grandfather's arms, and a "Baby's First Christmas" ornament I found tucked into the toe of my stocking, just as I'd found the "Our First Christmas" ornament a year before. Jackson had her name—Sara Joy Morgan—engraved on the back along with her date of birth—July 31, 1999.

Later that day, with the Christmas tree up and well lit, the time had come for me to pull out all of my carefully stored treasures. By midafternoon I sat on the floor with the ornament bins before me, cradling and fingering the keepsake commemorating Sara's first Yuletide holiday, half wondering when my children would return home and half hoping they'd give me a little more time alone with my thoughts. And with the tears that threatened to spill any second. I closed my eyes against the flurry of emotions and clutched the white baby-shoes-shaped ornament tied off with white ribbon and pink pearls.

How had someone who had come as such a shock to us at first become such a blessing later?

CHAPTER FIVE

Jackson and I met in kindergarten. If we met before that, neither of us could remember. Once we entered elementary school, we always seemed to have the same classroom or homeroom teacher.

But we had never been *friends,* really. We'd been *friendly,* but we'd never run in the same crowds. Then, in tenth grade, my best friend Callie encouraged me to try out for cheerleading with her. We both made the squad, which placed us in a different league from before. We'd gone from "smart girls only" to "smart *and* athletic."

Junior year, Jackson made quarterback, and I advanced to co-captain. After home games we'd all head to our favorite local café for burgers and fries. In short order, Jackson and I made a natural progression toward each other . . . sitting side by side in the booth, followed by him driving me home.

Jackson had always been a gentleman; we "dated" for two months before he kissed me, and that had been nothing more than a nervous peck. I remember saying to Callie during one of our gab sessions that for such a "big man on campus," Jackson sure was slow to make a move.

"Maybe he respects you," she said.

"Yeah," I answered. "Maybe."

"Monica Craig and I were talking before French II the other day. She goes to church with him. She says he's very involved over at First Methodist. President of his youth fellowship group. Actually has his lessons done for their Sunday school class. Teacher thinks he's all that and a slice of bread."

"Monica Craig," I all but snarled. "Now there's a piece of work."

"I'm not trying to start anything. I'm just telling you what she said."

As much as I didn't like Monica—and I had my reasons—she had been right about Jackson. That same year our two youth groups began having outings together—bonfires and cookouts and those kinds of things—and I witnessed firsthand how much Jackson's faith meant to him. When my mother was diagnosed with an aggressive form of breast cancer and died less than three months later, Jackson held me in his massive arms, pressing my face against his chest and breathing words of comfort from God's Word into my ear, reminding me that God had Mom, that I had him, and that Dad had me. And, with God, none of us were ever truly separated, even by death.

By senior year, when the University of Georgia had their eyes on Jackson and I'd made captain of the cheerleading squad, he and I were an exclusive item. We even alternated Sundays going to each other's church. Through it all, Jackson remained a gentleman.

Sure enough, UGA got Jackson, just as we all knew they would, and we celebrated around Callie's pool with a cookout, whooping it up until we were nearly dizzy. My mind instantly formulated plans, big plans. Jackson and I would attend UGA together. Become engaged over the Christmas holidays of our junior year. Marry after graduation. Jackson would possibly go on to have a pro career while I worked in some field of judicial law—I had yet to decide exactly which one. I only knew that the law excited me and that I found the smells within the courthouse—the few times I'd been inside—heady.

Jackson and I would wait a few years, of course, but we'd have a house full of children. And we'd grow old together . . . .

But when the university's scholarship offer to me came up short compared to Georgia Southern's, I'd been nothing shy of devastated. Dad, in some effort to soften the blow, quickly reminded me that with GSU being closer to home, he wouldn't have to worry about me as much. In a quiet moment he said words that would eventually come back to haunt me. "You and Jackson need some time apart anyway, Felicia. The two of you can't know what's out there beyond yourselves until you do."

I nodded, pretending to agree. But I couldn't see it. Not then, anyway.

Jackson, on the other hand, understood Dad's wisdom with a maturity beyond his years. Instead of commiserating with me, he again held me. Comforted me. "We've got to trust God's path for us, Leesha," he said, his lips against the crown of my head.

"I know . . . but I had—I had other plans."

I could feel his smile, and I nestled my face into his chest. "Oh, yeah? And what were those?"

I couldn't say the words. My mother would have rolled over in her grave if I'd told a boy—any boy—that I had imagined us married. Raising a family. Welcoming grandchildren. "Never mind."

He held me tighter, then pulled back, his eyes catching mine. "Listen, Leesha. I know we'll be a long way apart . . . don't cry, okay? Please don't."

But I couldn't help it. The tears fell like a sudden summer's rain, and he caught them with his thumbs. "I don't care how many miles are between UGA and Southern, you're my girl. And you always will be. You believe that, don't you?"

I nodded. Because I did. Until . . .

Later, when I accepted GSU's offer, we celebrated, but clearly not at the same level as we'd done for Jackson.

Goodness knows Jackson and I attempted to hold our relationship together. Whenever he came back to Bakersville, I drove home from Statesboro. We emailed every day and talked on the phone as often as we could. But by the spring of our freshman years—after a lovely Christmas holiday together—we realized our relationship couldn't withstand our personal changes, much less the distance.

The following summer we managed to see each other a few times, but by then Monica Craig had, once again, set her sights on Jackson. And for the first time, he seemed equally as interested in her.

"I wouldn't let it bother me," Callie said then. "Just chalk it up to the fact that he was a high school crush and nothing more."

I shook my head in answer because, truth was, it *did* bother me, and Jackson had been way more than a high school crush. He'd been—Callie aside—my best friend. He'd been my rock during the worst days of my life and now it seemed . . . "It just seems that he's throwing everything away for her."

"What do you mean?"

I snarled again, something I always did whenever Monica's name came up. "Monica is not the kind of girl who settles for a platonic relationship. Jackson may have always been a good guy with me, but you know Monica . . . "

"Oh." Callie pulled her shoulder-length curly blond hair into a haphazard ponytail with a scrunchie. "I get it. No matter what you say, you're jealous."

"I'm not," I said. "I just don't like seeing Jackson throw everything away."

But the truth was, I'd been holding onto a modicum of pride that Jackson and I had remained "pure." There was something to be said about being so powerfully attracted to another human being, especially in the midst of current moral dictates that went against that grain.

Now, between the two of us, I stood alone.

And, by the end of the summer, I'd only seen Jackson a handful of times. And each time, he and Monica seemed molded into each other, and, each time, he seemed a little more embarrassed by it. Then, in early August, Callie brought me the poolside news that Monica and her family had gone to Los Angeles to get her settled in an off-campus apartment.

"Apparently, she's been accepted to some design school," Callie said, grinning.

"So?"

"So?" She widened her hazel eyes at me. "So you've got two weeks before classes start to try to get him back."

I laughed. "I don't *want* him back," I said. "You're not following me, Callie. I'm doing well in school. I love where my studies are going, and I'm not looking for another boyfriend."

Callie threw her hands up. "Then what? What's with all the pitiful puppy eyes this summer?"

I squeezed some sunblock into the palm of my hand and slathered it on my shoulders, warmed by the hour I'd already spent lying next to our backyard pool. "I've just hated seeing him give up his strong faith for *Monica*."

Callie reached for the tube of sunblock and, wordless, opened it for herself. "I think we should drop the subject of Jackson Morgan."

I agreed.

But in October Callie called me and said his name again. "Leesha," she said, her voice strained. "I had to call you. Have you talked to your dad?"

My skin prickled. "No. What? Is Dad all right?"

"Yes, yes . . . it's Jackson's dad. He—he just dropped dead today at the store. Right there in front of the customers. My mom took some things over to the Morgans' and said that Jackson is on his way back from Athens."

"No . . ." I breathed out. "Jackson worships his father, Callie. He's going to be devastated."

"I thought you might want to know. Mrs. Morgan told Mom that a friend of Jackson's is driving him—that he's too distraught to drive himself."

I left Southern within the hour, headed straight for Bakersville, and called Dad along the way. He'd already been at the Morgans' as well. "Jackson is there," he said. "And he's pretty tore up."

"Oh, Dad." My heart hurt for Jackson, and I wanted desperately to be there for him as he'd been there for me when Mom passed away. "I'm going to go straight to Jackson's then, okay?"

"Just come on home when you can."

I drove the rest of the way remembering . . . and, mile by mile, letting go of my jealous anger that Jackson seemed to have so easily forgotten enough of our relationship to begin one with Monica Craig. That man no longer existed. Instead, I only saw the sweet boy of my youth. The one who'd held on to his morals. The one who'd cared so much for me in my moments of greatest sorrow. He had been everything to me then. I could do no less now than be everything for him.

As soon as I walked through the Morgans' kitchen door, Jackson's mother gave me a quick hug and told me that Jackson was up in his room. I'd never been in Jackson's bedroom, but I wove through the visitors and eased up the stairs and then down a dark hallway until I came to a closed bedroom door. I tapped lightly, then pressed my lips close and said, "Jackson?"

A moment later the door opened and a stranger stood before me. "Are you a friend?"

I peered past the hulk to see Jackson dressed in sweats and a tee as though he'd driven back home straight from practice, sprawled face-down on the rumpled cover of his bed. "You must be Jackson's friend."

He pointed to me. "Yeah. And I know who you are. You're Felicia."

I blinked. "Leesha."

The hulk pulled me into the room as he stepped into the hallway. "Maybe you can help him. He's pretty messed up right now." He glanced toward Jackson. "I'll leave you two alone," he said, then closed the door.

I stepped closer to Jackson, whose face was pressed into the pillow as he sobbed uncontrollably. "Jackson," I whispered as I climbed onto the bed beside him, keeping one foot on the floor. "Jackson? I'm here. I'm here."

He rolled over, and I peered into his eyes, their lashes drenched by tears, his lips swollen and his face splotched. "Leesha," he breathed out my name, and drew me into his arms.

I stretched out beside him. "I'm here," I said again, my arms wrapping around his shoulders as I tried to draw him into the same comfort he'd given me when Mom died. I buried my face into his neck, warm and spice-scented. "I'm here," I said a final time.

And then the world turned on its axis.

❄

Less than two months later, in early December, I called Jackson and asked if I could drive up to Athens to see him. To talk to him about something. He stuttered around my request, then said, "Sure, okay. I've got—well, how about Saturday?"

I don't know if Jackson realized immediately my reason for visiting, but by the time I'd driven the three-and-a-half hours and found the restaurant Jackson suggested, he'd put one and one together and arrived at three. And by the middle of that month, at the end of fall semester, Jackson dropped out of school to keep his father's auto parts store going for his mother, and I had dropped out of Southern to marry him in hopes of wiping the look of disappointment from the face of my father.

CHAPTER SIX

Christmas Season 2018

The children arrived home by six thirty, Hank nearly beside himself with stories of the decorations gracing Nana's house.

I gave him a tight hug. "Hungry?"

"We had lunch *and* supper with Daddy," he said.

I kissed his cheek. "Go upstairs and brush your teeth then."

Travis stood next to the tree, admiring the infinitesimal amount of work I'd done in their absence. "Looking good, Mom." He lightly flicked the "Our First Christmas" ornament with the tip of his index finger. "At least you got the first one up."

"I also got the second one up," I noted, pointing to the Baby's First Christmas ornament. "What do you think? Will it be as good as Nana's when I'm done?" I teased, knowing full well no one decorated a tree like my mother-in-law.

"Yeah," he drawled, letting me know the obvious. Something tumbled upstairs, and he pointed toward the ceiling. "I'd better go help Hank."

I joined Sara, who sat on the sofa. "Dad says hi."

I forced a smile. "That's nice," I said, raising my brow. "He's doing well, I take it?"

She nodded. "For the most part." She took a breath. "And Nana says please don't be a stranger."

"I'll call her."

Sara grabbed my hand. "Dad misses you, Mom."

Tears formed, hot and threatening. "How do you know that, Sara?" I asked around the traitorous knot in my throat.

"I can tell."

"Did he *say* he misses me? Did he ask about me at all?"

"Yes," she said, but her eyes only grazed mine.

"What did he say?" I challenged. "Exactly."

The look on her face told me she wasn't happy about being put in the "word for word" middle. "He asked how you were doing and we told him about the tree and he said he knows how much you enjoy this time of the year." She squeezed my hand again. "Mom, your anniversary is right around the corner. Seriously now, you two *have* to get your acts together. Both of you. Wasn't Thanksgiving bad enough?"

I turned toward her, pulling my hand from hers. "I'm not the one who left, and I'm not the one who made no move toward spending Thanksgiving together."

She shook her head. "I cannot talk to you about this. I'm the last person on the face of this planet who should, but honestly, Mom, when are you *ever* going to give him a break? Or yourself?"

"Is that what he said? That this is my fault?"

"No. He didn't say *anything*. Mom, he doesn't talk to me about the details. Ever. But I can read the look on his face, and I—I can hear it in his voice. He *misses* you, Mom."

"He doesn't call . . ." He'd even managed to keep all the visitation details between himself and the kids, I suppose to keep as much distance between the two of us as possible. And, in turn, to lessen the chances for arguing. He didn't even bother to come inside when he brought Travis home from his afternoon shifts at Morgan's. Nor did he wave from behind the steering wheel.

"Would you talk to him if he did?"

"I don't know," I answered honestly. "I mean, of course I'd *talk* to him, but I—"

"He loves you, Mom. And you love him. You know you do." She stood. Started for the foyer door and the staircase. "Like I said, you just need to give yourself a break."

I squeezed my hand into a fist and watched her walk up the stairs until her feet disappeared into nothing but sound above my head. I glanced at the ceiling, noting the ornate crown molding and remembered our first real home, purchased shortly after our second Christmas.

❄

January 2000

Jackson spotted the Craftsman-style home on his way to work one shivering morning shortly after the New Year. "A detour," he told me when he got home. "And so I'm winding my way between Georgia Avenue and Baker's to get to the alleyway behind the store and there it was with a FOR SALE sign that practically has our names written all over it."

I stood in the studio's kitchenette, stirring Italian beans with one hand and holding Sara on my hip with the other as he rambled on about window boxes and a white picket fence. "Perfect for us," he continued.

"Do you know how much it is?" I asked, dropping the slotted spoon into an odds-and-ends dessert plate I used for a rest and then handing our daughter to her father. "Your turn," I said.

Jackson nuzzled our six-month-old, planting raspberries into the folds of her neck. "Miss me?" he asked, and she giggled in pure delight.

So far, our daughter seemed to lean more toward being her father's child than mine, despite my adoring her with my whole heart. "Jackson," I said, claiming his attention again. "How much?"

"Sixty-eight-eight," he answered as though he'd just said sixty-eight dollars rather than sixty-eight thousand.

My mouth opened and, for a moment, nothing came out. "Can we afford that?"

Jackson shifted Sara from one arm to the next, then leaned against the sink counter. "I've not said anything—you know I don't like to brag—but, Leesha, I've taken Dad's store and really done something with it. We're making a good profit now."

I turned off the burners and reached for two plates in the cabinet next to Jackson's head, which he tilted to the opposite direction. "I always thought your father did pretty well." I shrugged. "I mean, based on—you know—the house you grew up in and . . ."

Jackson smiled. "Well, that house came from money on Mom's side of the family."

I clutched the plates to my chest. "I didn't know that."

"Not something Dad was overly proud of. It didn't keep him from enjoying Mom's inheritance, and he was good when it came to their personal investments, but the store barely made a profit every year."

I walked to the tiny table and set the plates down. "I guess that's better than going into the red."

"It is, but Leesh—we're way in the black now. I'm making a pretty good salary and we've got the money to make the mortgage payments."

Sara reached for me. I scooped her out of Jackson's arms, then walked her to the tiny living area and placed her in the playpen her nana had given us as a baby gift. After shaking a rattle and then leaving it with her, I started the process of taking the pots and pans from the kitchen to the table, preparing the plates, and then back again.

"You know," Jackson said, "if you prepared them *in* the kitchen, you wouldn't have to go back and forth."

I pointed the spoon at him. "Do you want this job?"

He held his hands up as if I were about to rob a bank. "I'm just trying to be helpful."

"Yeah . . . well . . ." I sat in my chair and motioned for Jackson to find his way to the one opposite mine. "Let's get back to the house."

Jackson sat, dwarfing the chair, the table, and everything in between. He said his customary grace, then drew his napkin into his left hand and held it there. "I've made an appointment for us to look at it. Tomorrow afternoon."

"What time?" I placed my napkin in my lap.

"Three. Work for you?"

"That's typically when Sara's napping."

Jackson looked surprised, as though Sara and I just sat around all day watching TV and eating ice cream. "I'll make it four. Does that work?"

I nodded. "Probably so."

Before I could process what we were doing, we purchased the house—an adorable three-bedroom, two-bath Craftsman with hardwood floors and arched doorways and built-ins and wallpapered walls Callie and I spent hours stripping. With that task behind us, we spent a few more hours at the local hardware store picking out paint, and with that done, we worked days on end with paint and roller brushes and long strips of tape. Every afternoon after work, Jackson stopped by to check on our progress, always giving "thumbs up" approval.

"You do good work for a couple of girls," he teased more than once, which always earned him a sock in the arm from Callie and a glare from me.

Callie, who worked as the administrator's assistant in our local nursing home, had begun to date an old schoolmate, Taylor Reddick, who'd graduated two classes ahead of us and who had returned home from Tifton with a degree from Abraham Baldwin Agricultural College. Together, the four of us spent an entire weekend shopping for and purchasing middle-of-the-road furniture and a top-of-the-line patio grill Jackson and Taylor declared would get its debut workout the very weekend we moved. Shy of the night of Sara's birth, this was the happiest I'd seen Jackson since the day I broke the news to him of her impending arrival and, for the briefest of moments, I allowed myself to relax enough to feel joy right along with him.

Or, if not joy, something close to contentment.

❄

Christmas Season 2018

As my children clomped along upstairs in their preparation for bed, I pulled one more item from the bin and remembered . . . that year—the year of the house purchase—the toe of my Christmas stocking boasted a Lenox "Our First Home" ornament, which I now took out of its protective box to hang on a nearly bare tree.

Chapter Seven

"It's Beginning to Look a Lot Like Christmas" played overhead as I stared across the café-styled table at the woman who'd seen me through nearly every moment of my life. After swiping cappuccino foam from my upper lip with the tip of my index finger, I said, "I think the kids want me to make a move toward having their dad come to the house for Christmas Day."

Callie's eyes met mine over a cup of steaming herbal tea. Its cinnamon scent drifted to me, and I inhaled deeply as she placed her mug back on the table. "What makes you think that?"

I shrugged. "Sara mostly. One liners. You know how she can get."

Callie crossed her arms. "She wants her parents back together." She bent forward. "And I don't mean for the holiday."

I retrieved the tiny spoon nestled between my cup and saucer, stirred my coffee for no good reason, and decided to change the subject. "What are you and Taylor and the kids doing this year?"

Callie sighed—an indicator she wasn't going to give up easily but that she would answer anyway. "It's Taylor's mother's turn," she said with a roll of her eyes.

I couldn't help but laugh. "See now?" I pointed at her. "*This* year I don't have to endure Mrs. Morgan's glares." I shook my head enough to toss the short waves of hair around my face. "Nice as she can be, I still get the feeling she looks at me and sees only the teenaged girl who forced her son out of college."

Callie took another sip of tea. "Oh, for the love of Pete. He was already packing to move back home the day you went to tell him about Sara. He'd already made his decision to leave school and keep the business afloat weeks before he even knew and—why am *I* reliving this? Especially right before Christmas? It's *your* angst to deal with."

I smiled. "Because you love me."

"That I do. Enough to circle back around . . ." She drew a curlicue in the air with her finger.

I groaned.

"Stop it. Fact is, you love Jackson and Jackson loves you so—"

"I'm not the one who left."

"Stop. It."

This time I crossed my arms and leaned forward. "What would you have me do, Callie? Run down to Morgan's and get on my knees, tell him he was right and I was wrong, and beg him to come home?"

Callie raised a brow, daring me to calm my nonsensical self down. "Would that solve your issues?"

I huffed. "*What* issues?"

She downed the last of her tea. "Darlin', if you don't know, I can't help you." She flip-flopped her hands in the air, a conductor orchestrating the conversation. "Not that you'd let anyone anyway."

It was my turn to sigh as she reached for her purse, planted in one of the empty seats beside her. "Are you leaving? Already? I don't have to pick up Hank from after-school care for another half hour."

She pulled up her sweater cuff to look at her watch. "Got to. I promised Benji and Allie I'd take them to Savannah this evening so they can do a little shopping for their dad and me . . . friends . . . grandparents . . ." She rolled her eyes again as she stood. "And you know what it's like shopping for Grandmother Reddick."

I attempted to stifle another chuckle. Poor Callie. No matter what she'd done in the sixteen years of her marriage to Taylor— including producing the most beautiful twins I'd ever seen and advancing to become the nursing home's administrator—her mother-in-law had treated her like no more than one of Taylor's casual girlfriends from his pre-Callie days. "You'll win her over one day," I said. "Mark my words."

"Oh, yeah? When?"

I reached for my purse as well. "When Bakersville produces snow on the Fourth of July." We headed for the door together.

"Listen," Callie said as we neared the curb where we'd parked our cars side-by-side. "Seriously. Think about calling Jackson. I believe he'd love to come over Christmas morning . . . see the kids open their gifts from Santa. Especially Hank. Not to mention Travis's birthday celebration." She grinned. "Maybe you could ask him over for Christmas *Eve* . . . you could *wake up together*?"

I slapped her arm playfully. "Now *you* stop it. *That* certainly won't solve our iss—" My words caught in my throat as a sudden movement of red slipped out of Hoffman's Jewelry Store across the street.

"What?" Callie asked, turning in the direction of my gaze. "Oh."

"Monica. Craig."

"Don't let her see you staring," she said, and I instantly looked first to my feet and then back to Callie's face. "*She* is not your issue either."

"Isn't she?" I asked.

"Oh, Leesh . . . when are you *ever* going to get it?"

A half hour later, Hank sat in his booster seat, hands clasped, eyes peering out the back-passenger window. "Mommy," he said as though he'd just exhaled the world's problems.

I glanced into the rearview mirror at him for the fifth time in as many minutes and watched the light from streetlamps play in his dark eyes. "What, darlin'?"

"I sure do hate going home these days."

A deep pang drove itself through my heart as I turned my attention back to the street. "But Mommy will soon have all the ornaments up on the tree, and you and Travis and Sara can string popcorn and hang the tinsel . . ." Which Sara had actually managed to find and had delivered before she'd even left to return to college on Sunday evening.

"But *Mommy*. The house is so quiet when we get home."

A glance at the dashboard clock told me we were forty-five minutes from Travis returning from his afternoon job at Morgan's.

"Mommy, when does Sara come home for good?" My youngest son's tone seemed so downcast, I almost pulled over to cry along with him.

"She has a few more days of classes, and then she'll be home until after New Year's Day. How does that sound?"

"It sounds good, I reckon, but when is Daddy coming home for good?"

I glanced into the rearview mirror again. "Honey, I—" The right words escaped me. Or the *other* right words. Hadn't I explained our separation to Hank well enough? "Listen. What's say you and I ride around and see if anyone has put out their Christmas lights yet? How does that sound?"

"Well . . ." he began, then said, "How about if you take me to Daddy's store, and I can ride home with Travis?"

"Honey, Daddy will bring Travis home shortly and—" And he would step out of the car to hug his youngest son but refuse to walk into his own home. What *used* to be his home.

"Mommy?" Hank repeated my name, his voice elevated and anxious and jarring me from my private tirade.

"Yes, my love."

"What are you and Daddy getting Travis for his birthday this year? 'Cause *I* know what he wants."

"Oh, do you now?" With the new change in subject, I decided to keep driving toward home. We were so close anyway.

"He wants a Jeep," Hank informed me, and I sputtered out laughter.

"Well, I'm afraid he's not getting a Jeep this year. He'll only be fourteen, which means he's got another two years before Daddy and I will think about buying him a car."

"Oh," Hank said by way of commentary as I pulled the car into our driveway. "Will you talk to Daddy when he brings Travis home tonight?"

I put the car in park. "I guess so," I said turning in time to see him unhook himself from his car seat. "For now, let's just get inside. It's getting colder by the minute."

"Travis says that one day he's going to get a Jeep and—" Hank opened the car door and hopped onto the driveway where he waited for me to reach him.

"And?" I asked, now more than a little curious.

Hank's expression grew serious. "And he's got *big* plans for it."

I smiled down at my son. "Well, we've all had big plans at one time or another . . ."

❄

Early June 2004

I stood over the bathroom counter, staring at the Clearblue Easy digital home pregnancy test I'd laid flat on a paper towel, then glanced at my watch.

Two more minutes.

"You'd better not have done this to me again, Jackson Morgan," I whispered toward the stick. "Not *now* anyway."

And not that I didn't absolutely adore my daughter. And not that I wouldn't welcome another baby. Just. Not. Now.

I crossed my arms against a nonexistent chill in the room and counted back to a weekend in late April. Jackson had talked his mother into spending two full days watching Sara while he whisked me off to Wilmington Island, where a charming waterfront cottage drenched in the shadows of dozens of live oaks awaited us. Jackson chattered the entire two-hour drive there, telling me that the house came with a sailboat and that we could take all day Saturday to cruise out of Wilmington River and into the Wassaw Sound. "Great for fishing too," he said, as if I were into that sort of thing.

"I tell you what," I said. "You go fishing, and I'll drink up the sunshine."

"I've got reservations for dinner tomorrow night at one of the finest seafood restaurants Savannah has to offer," he said. "Candlelight and live music. Taylor told me about it . . . it's going to be real nice."

His ears blushed in that way I'd grown accustomed to, the way that told me he had more than fishing and seafood on his mind. To divert the subject, I threw in, "I was thinking, Jackson . . ."

He reached over the console of our Nissan Altima and took my hand. "Yeah?"

"Sara starts school in the fall . . ."

"I know. Can you believe it? Our baby growing up so fast? I've decided, Leesha. I'm taking off that day. The whole day. I want to be there when she walks in for the first time." He glanced at me. "I know she's been going to kindergarten this past year, but that's not really the same. I want to *be* there when she walks into the same school you and I went to as first graders."

I furrowed my brow as I crossed one leg over the other, feeling more trapped by his announcement than excited. "And you need to take the whole day off for that?"

"No, but I thought that maybe you and I could go have breakfast or an early lunch. Spend the day together . . . you know . . ."

Yeah. I knew.

"Well, school *is* what I want to talk about. Just not Sara's." I took a deep breath, then exhaled as fast as my lungs allowed. "Jackson, I want to go back to college."

CHAPTER EIGHT

Christmas Season 2018

While Hank washed up for supper, I searched the ornament bin for the Wilmington Island ornament Jackson had placed in my stocking that year. The one I'd not pulled out of my stocking until several days after Christmas. Finding it, I took it out of its box and then searched for the right branch near the top of the tree to hang it from.

I stood back. The delicate ball shimmered in the lights Hank turned on before heading upstairs, its blue and white snowflakes made all the more magical against the deep green of the tree. I smiled.

I'd not been able to go back to college that year—morning sickness gripped me with a fury I'd not experienced with Sara. On Christmas morning, as everyone else in Bakersville tore into their gifts, I pushed my second born into the world. Jackson stood beside me, holding my hand and breathing heavily as I gritted my teeth and heaved one final time.

I remembered looking at his face as I fell back against the pillow, hearing Travis's first cries echoing through the labor room. Jackson, drenched in beads of perspiration, cried out, "I have a *son*. We have a Christmas Day baby boy!"

Dr. Medlock brought the baby to my chest, then prepared Jackson for cutting the cord as I held on to the squirmy offspring of a weekend getaway. My heart leapt beneath his tiny head, and I brought my lips to the tender crown, thinking—wildly—that not for nothing, when Jackson and I abandoned ourselves to the moment and any shred of good sense—or at the very least, planning—I always ended up falling in love nine months after.

Now, almost fourteen years later, I was more madly in love than I could have begun to imagine then. Travis had given me a difficult pregnancy, but he'd been nothing but a wonderful child. As young adulthood shouted from the whiskers springing out on his chin and upper lip, and in the ways he had begun to fill out like his father, he continued to bless me.

To bless us.

Hank breezed back into the living room as lights from Jackson's truck cut through the dark driveway outside and through the house. I peered beyond the tree boughs to see the silhouettes of my husband and our son in the cab. Travis had his head turned toward his father, his mouth moving within the glow of the streetlamp. No telling what he rambled on about.

"Daddy's here," Hank bellowed as he tore out of the room for the front door.

"Hank, don't run," I shouted behind him seconds before the door rattled shut.

The truck stopped, and both Jackson and Travis stepped out, Jackson reaching for Hank as he jumped into his arms. Travis made it halfway to the steps, throwing his hand up in a good-bye wave while Jackson continued to hold Hank, speaking to him for a moment.

The front door opened and Travis called out.

"In here," I said, still watching the display of affection in my driveway.

"Dad says to tell you hey and . . ."

I moved past him, dismissing whatever he had to say. Because I had something to say. Namely that we were a family and families spend Christmas together. Especially when birthdays and anniversaries come at the same time.

" . . . and where are you going?"

"I'll be right back."

"He says he wants to—" Travis began but I shut the front door, cutting off the rest of his sentence.

The cold night air hit hard enough for me to wrap my arms around myself as I went down the front porch steps. "Hank," I said, "Baby, you need a coat."

Jackson, dressed in form-fitting jeans and a Morgan's long-sleeved tee and ballcap, looked up as Hank glanced over his shoulder. "Daddy's got me, Mommy. And Daddy's warm."

Oh, yes. I remembered. Jackson never got cold and, when I was, he'd pull me into his arms until the heat of him reached my bones. I nearly tripped over the memory until Jackson spoke up. "Did Travis tell you I wanted to talk with you?"

"Ah—no," I said, stopping a good two feet from him.

Jackson returned Hank to the driveway. "Get on inside, son," he said. "Daddy'll see you tomorrow, okay?"

"But I—"

"Go on, now," he said, his voice gentle. "I need to talk to Mommy about some things."

Hank took his sweet time as Jackson's eyes followed him into the house. When the door finally closed, I said, "You needed to talk to me?"

Jackson spread his legs and crossed his arms in a "coach-on-the-sidelines" manner. His blue eyes found mine from beneath the visor of the cap, and for a moment my heart quickened. Time had been nothing but good to Jackson Morgan. He'd met the beginning of middle age with determination, working out more, eating better.

I squared my shoulders and sucked in my slight I've-had-three-children stomach at the sight of him.

"You look nice," Jackson said. "I always liked that color pink on you."

I looked down and pulled at the hem of my sweater. "Thank you."

"Look, Leesh, we need to talk about Christmas."

"I know. I—"

"I mean, *really* talk about it."

I looked over my shoulder at the house, specifically at the living room window where I felt certain our two sons stood watching. "I—yeah, I know," I said looking again at Jackson. "I wanted to—Callie thinks—" I stopped myself. No way would I tell him what Callie thought.

"Callie?" he chuckled. "Callie's always got an opinion."

"And usually a good one," I countered, my dander rising.

"I'm not arguing," he said, throwing his hands up.

"Did I say you were arguing?"

He crossed his arms again, his lips now in a thin line. "Let's not fight, Felicia."

"No, by all means." How had the mood changed so quickly? The air grown so much more biting? "All right. Christmas." I took the chance and said, "Would you like to come over Christmas morning? I was thinking early enough for us to see the kids open their gifts."

He blew warm air from his lungs, condensation forming smoke around his face. "Actually, I was thinking I could come get them Christmas Eve morning. Spend the day with them. Take them to Mom's for Christmas Eve dinner. Bring them home after that."

I blinked in astonishment. "It's our year to take them to Dad's for Christmas Eve."

"*We* don't have years to divvy up anymore," he countered quickly. "Remember?"

"Because *you* left—"

"Because *you* couldn't stand to have me here anymore, Leesha. You were making life imposs—" He shook his head. "Look," he said with a point. "I want my children on Christmas Eve." One brow cocked. "Hear me?"

I looked up and down the street. "Yes, I hear you, Jackson, and I'm sure so do the neighbors."

"Then I suggest you go inside." He reached for the door handle. "Because this conversation is over."

Chapter Nine

After dinner—after dishes had been done and Hank had taken his bath and said his bedtime prayers—I crawled onto the king-size four-poster rice bed that seemed to grow larger with each passing night. I reached to the bedside table where my cell phone charged, then called a number I knew as well as my own.

"Felicia?" an older woman's voice queried.

"Hey, Treva," I said to the office manager of Langford, Hancock and Associates, which also happened to be where I worked. Treva was also the woman who'd introduced me to a Bible study group I'd been with for several years. The sixty-three-year-old loved the BBC as much as her husband loved ESPN. "I could use some advice," I admitted. "And some prayer."

"I figured as much at this late hour." Her voice held a slight British accent.

"Oh. Did I call at a bad time? What are you watching?"

"*Keeping Up Appearances,* but I'm never too busy for you. Besides, I was nearing the end of an episode. Ronny's watching one of his sports thingies, so I was about to either go into another or set the house on fire. I just can't decide which."

I chuckled. Treva had a way of pouring out words and wisdom that made me feel as though she somehow channeled my mother. Not that I believed in things like that.

Treva and Ronny Hicks had been married longer than I'd been alive. Unable to have children, they'd made the young people of their church their offspring . . . and that included me.

"Jackson wants the children Christmas Eve," I told her.

"And?"

"*All day.*"

"They are his children too, Felicia." Since we'd met, Treva refused to call me by anything other than my given name.

"I know, but this is Dad's year to have . . ." I stopped. "This has nothing to do with my father though, does it?"

"No, it doesn't."

My shoulders sank. "Oh, Treva. What am I going to do?" I almost couldn't bear the thought of the kids with Jackson but without me the day before Christmas. Not to mention the day after our anniversary. And especially considering that my mind had already entertained notions of Monica being there as well.

"My darling," she said after a pause, "this has nothing to do with Christmas and everything to do with you and Jackson."

"I know," I whispered.

"Will you allow me a few words here?"

I straightened. "Of course. That's why I called."

"I've tried to stay out of this . . . I even told Ronny I've nearly bit a hole straight through my tongue."

"Mmm . . ."

"Ronny and I married when I was twenty and he twenty-one, and with enough stars in our eyes to light up the night. Nineteen seventy-five was a pretty good year as far as years go. Everything free and easy. I'd gone to a business college and Ronny had taken drafting at the same school, and we both had pretty good jobs. We could easily save money and one day have children, and we'd spend the rest of our days loving each other and them. Building a family. A home."

She paused, perhaps waiting for me to say something. But I didn't know what to say. Jackson and I hadn't had such moments. We'd been thrown together by a sorrow-filled night that led to actions neither of us had been prepared for, followed by two parents and a pastor intent on seeing us "do the right thing" nearly as much as we'd been intent on the same.

"So, anyway," she continued, "as you know . . . the children never came. I started having health issues right away, and within two years I had to have a complete hysterectomy."

"I didn't know . . ."

"I know you didn't. Most folks don't. When I was old enough to have children, people asked when I would. And then, when I was too old, they asked questions like, 'And you never had children?' as though having them was some sort of requirement."

"People can be cruel."

"Not on purpose, of course. But yes. Let me tell you something, Felicia. Ronny and I had big dreams. Some of them came true. Some didn't. We've had twice as many good times as bad, but that didn't make the bad times any less severe."

"I know . . ."

"But at the center of it all was the Lord. *He is before all things, and in him all things hold together.* Colossians 1:17."

I smiled at how quickly she inserted the reference but added, "Jackson and I go to church, Treva. We've raised our children there . . . we're believers . . ."

"My darling," she repeated the endearment. "I have only one thing to add and it's a question, really, because it's at the center of the center."

"Okay."

"What was the last thing Jesus said in the Lord's Prayer? The last thing He told His disciples?"

"Amen?"

"Cute. But wrong. Look it up. Ponder it. Matthew's version, not Luke's."

"Okay. I will. I'll look it up shortly."

"You do that. Then we'll talk . . ."

I intended to look up the verses in Matthew the following morning during my quiet time, but the quiet time didn't come. I overslept instead, the events of the previous evening having woken me intermittently during the night, robbing me of my rest and reminding me of my shortcomings.

I may not have been the best wife to Jackson, but I had worrying down to a science.

The house was a flurry of "hurry ups" and "let's go" that morning, with me foregoing my usual cup of decaf and, instead, brewing a cup of Sara's caffeinated, which I took to the car in a travel mug and almost left on the hood.

I managed to get both Travis and Hank to their individual schools and myself to the office before Treva declared me officially late.

"Something tells me," she said while standing over my desk with her dark-skinned arms crossed and one foot tapping the hardwood floor, "you didn't sleep so well last night." Her words rang with far more love and concern than rebuke, which may have been the only thing keeping me from tumbling over the edge.

"What gave it away?" I asked, pulling open the right bottom drawer in my desk and shoving my purse into it.

She grinned at me, and tiny wrinkles made their way up the sides of her face. "You're not wearing makeup."

I slapped my hands against my cheeks. "Oh, you're kidding."

Treva laughed as merriment played in her black eyes. "Don't worry. You're not the first face folks see when they walk in the front door . . ."

I pulled the middle drawer of my desk out, retrieved a small mirror I kept there, and stared at my reflection in disbelief. "I can't believe I remembered to brush my hair but I forgot to put on makeup. I can only hope *the boys* don't need me to run to the courthouse for anything today."

"Did you at least brush your teeth?"

"Oh, Treva . . . really. Of course."

"And did you read the verses in Matthew?"

I grimaced, remembering that worse than forgetting to put on makeup had been losing my quiet time with God by oversleeping. "No. But I will . . . I promise."

Treva clapped her hands together once, then pivoted toward the door leading from my office and into the hallway. "Well, let's get to it," she said, which is what she said every morning to each of us legal secretaries. "Oh," she said, turning just outside the door. "Remember that necklace you saw up at Vanessa's? The one you thought Sara would like for Christmas?"

"The Ginger Snaps necklace?"

"Mmm . . . Vanessa put her entire collection on sale yesterday."

I gasped with delight. "Oooh . . . I'll head up there during my lunch. Once she puts them on sale, those things sell out nearly as fast as she puts them out."

"Well, for all that is sacred, don't forget to wear sunglasses."

"Why?"

"Helps to hide the fact that you didn't—" She drew a circle in the air around her face as she fought to keep from laughing.

"Oh, very funny," I teased back, even as I hoped my oversized shades were in the car.

Chapter Ten

I dashed into Vanessa's during my lunch hour, immediately intoxicated by the holiday music and scents, the festive décor, and the adorable clothes hanging from lightly-scented hangers near the entrance. I shoved my sunglasses to the crown of my head, caught a good look at myself in a wall mirror, and immediately drew them back to the bridge of my nose. Spying a medium-sized, shapely 1.4.3. Story blouse on the rack, I snagged it, then walked to a corner where a gilded floor mirror leaned against the wall.

With the sunglasses still on, holding the blouse up to my body told me nothing, so I drew them up again, causing my medium-length hair to stick out at all angles. Still, the top's maroon fabric blended well with my skin tone, so I threw it over my arm before making my way to the back of the store where Vanessa kept her jewelry.

"Oh," Vanessa—a petite, young, go-getting entrepreneur—greeted me from behind the jewelry counter. "You look—I almost didn't recog—"

I threw my hand up in a dismissal. "I know. I overslept. No time for fixing myself up," I said in a tone that suggested this to be a common and perfectly acceptable occurrence.

"Oh," Vanessa said again, blinking her perfectly-lined doe-eyes at me as her pink-tinted lips pursed. "Well," she finally said with a sigh. "How can I help you, Miss Felicia?"

I pulled a necklace from the display rack and held it up. "I want to get this for Sara for Christmas," I said, extending it. "Plus a few of the snaps."

Vanessa took the necklace. "Good timing. I just put them on sale."

"I heard."

"Great. Well, then. I'll get a box," she said. "Take your time looking in the little cubbies there." She paused. "Do you want me to hold that top for you?"

I nodded as I handed her the blouse, then peered down at the display of jeweled snaps designed for the necklace, picking up one or two of them and holding them at eye level as the door chimes sent a musical hello to another patron.

"Vanessa," a voice called from behind me. "I'm in a terrible hurry . . . do you have my—"

I turned in time to see Monica Craig waltzing in, thick russet-colored hair pulled back in a slick ponytail that swung with each step. She wore winter-white wool slacks, a mid-thigh length Christmas-red sweater that accentuated her willowy lines, and leather ankle boots. The deep almond of her eyes was accentuated by the black liner drawn to perfection around them and the thick lashes that nearly reached Audrey Hepburn brows.

Seeing me, she paused, a cat-like grin spreading across her glossy lips. "Well, hello, Leesha," she said. "Fancy meeting you here."

I turned back to the display, biting my lips in hopes of bringing a modicum of color to dead-peach tone, then turned again. The grin hadn't left.

"Are you buying a necklace for yourself or—" she asked.

"For Sara," I said, hoping to remind her that Jackson and I shared three children.

She ducked her chin just so as her eyes widened. "Oh, yes . . ." Then she tilted her head ever-so-slightly and added, "Did you just wake up or something?"

"No, I—"

Blessedly, Vanessa returned to the counter before I could finish. "Oh, hey, Miss Monica. I set that top aside for you. A small, right?"

"Naturally."

"I'll be right back. I kept it in my office."

I pretended to continue in my search for the perfect snaps as Vanessa walked farther into the back and Monica sidled up next to me. "You know, when I lived in L.A. I had all sorts of shops to go to. Now, with only one . . . but Vanessa has an adorable selection to choose from." She sighed with a flare of drama on the side. "Thank goodness."

I forced a smile. "Well, if you can't find it here, there's always online shopping. I hear Amazon sells more than just books . . . everything from books to bras."

Monica's mouth dropped open. "Wha—"

"Here you go, Miss Monica," Vanessa said, returning. "Is this the one you want?"

Monica beamed with delight. "It's exactly the one I want," she said, plopping her Dooney and Bourke bag on the counter in front of her. "Let me get the AMEX for you . . ."

I slammed the drawer that housed the selection of snaps, having chosen five to go with the necklace.

"I'll be right with you, Miss Felicia," Vanessa said, turning to me with a smile. "Soon as I ring Miss Monica up." A shift in customer service that left me close to furious.

And I still fumed as, a half hour later, I explained to Treva what had happened.

"And she had chosen the same blouse as you?" she asked from behind her desk, mirth nearly changing the color of her eyes.

"It's not funny," I remarked, trying hard not to laugh, even a little, at her. "And I have to get back to work."

"Wait. Wait," she said in a vain attempt at becoming serious. "You didn't say . . . did you buy the blouse or not?"

Crossing my arms, I said, "I most assuredly did not."

Treva shook her head. "That is rich. It really is."

"And of all the days for her to see me . . ." I said, as if the thought had just come to my mind.

She leaned her forearms on her desk and sobered. "Sweetheart, now I want you to listen to me right now. Monica Craig is not your problem."

"You don't know—"

"Yes, I do. Jackson Morgan is no more having an affair with Monica Craig than Ronny Hicks is. You can put that notion right out of you mind."

"You are a wise woman, Treva, but you don't *know* that." I sighed deeply. "Not that I for one second think he did anything, you know, *wrong* with her while he was still at home. But he's been gone since the summer and men—"

"Men, nothing." She pointed her manicured index finger up as if to make a final point. "That boy loves you, Felicia."

I started for the door leading out of her office and into the hallway of the early 1900s rambling Victorian that housed the law office. "Does he, Treva?"

"Stop right there," she ordered, and I did, turning to face her from beneath the door's dormer window. "He. Does."

"I know you mean well. I do. But, you didn't hear him last night . . ." I looked to the wool carpet gracing the rich, dark wood of the floor. "And you weren't—you don't know . . ." I raised my chin. "There's so much more than you can understand." I shook my head, letting her know the conversation had come to an end. "I'm sorry. I have to get back to work."

Chapter Eleven

With it being Tuesday, I found myself looking at only four more evenings to get the remainder of *the* ornaments on the tree, what with Sara due home for the holidays sometime that Saturday afternoon. Under ordinary circumstances and in any other year, the work would have come easily. It would have been done already. Within minutes.

For nearly as many years as we'd been married, I'd placed the keepsakes from Jackson on select branches before any others could be hung, a tradition whose beginnings dated back to our third Christmas together.

❄

December 2000

With Sara sporting a cold, Jackson had gone alone to Steadman's to purchase our first Fraser fir, then wrestled it from the truck into the tiny living room of the Craftsman.

Once he'd gotten it into its stand, I stared up at where the top bent against the ceiling in protest. "It's too tall," I said.

"Nah," Jackson countered. "The ceiling's just too low."

"And it's too . . . *fat*. Look at it, Jackson. It nearly takes up the whole room." Jackson started to comment, but I stopped him with, "And don't tell me the room is too small."

He chuckled. "I think I overdid it."

I waved my arms in exasperation. "Jackson, I can't believe you got one so big. What in blue blazes do you think we're going to put on this tree? We have two ornaments. Two."

His arms circled me from behind, pinning mine to the sides of my body. "Would you relax, please," he asked, nuzzling my neck. He'd grown a cropped beard, the hair of it so blond it nearly blended with his skin, but bristly enough to send shivers down my legs when he tried to kiss me.

Or in times like these.

"Jackson . . . Sara will be up from her nap soon . . ."

But he continued with the nibbling, mumbling, "So?"

Somehow, I managed to have enough presence of mind to break away. "Can we stay on the subject, please?"

My husband plopped onto our new overstuffed sofa with dramatic flair. "Why are you making this complicated?"

I stepped closer to the tree, breathed in the fresh scent of it and forced myself not to think back to the evening we'd stood in Pastor Evan and Miss Arlene's living room. Or of the following night, when Jackson had given me the first ornament. Or later . . . "I'm not," I said. "Seriously, Jackson . . . no, seriously, wait right there." I pointed at him, then went into our bedroom closet to retrieve the box housing one of our two ornaments. I hung "Our First Christmas" in the center of the massive greenery. "Look. Pure silly. And Sara's baby's first Christmas memento isn't going to make it much better."

Jackson stood, reaching for me in one fluid move. He grabbed my fisted hand and pulled me back to the sofa, landing me on his lap. Again, his arms circled me, pulling me to him, forcing me to his whims. "Would. You. Stop," he said, drawing me close. "I'll have you know there is this new invention called a store . . ." He kissed my jaw and I flinched. "You may have heard of it . . . where you can buy all sorts of things. Garland . . . ornaments . . . plain ones, fancy ones . . ."

I couldn't help myself; I relaxed in his embrace under the onslaught of his kisses. "But I always wanted the ornaments on my tree to have special meaning."

"Like what," he asked, pushing my hair from my face before planting another kiss on the tip of my nose.

"Jackson," I breathed. "You know . . . like the ones Sara will make one day in Sunday school and kindergarten . . ."

"Well, she'll have to grow up a little bit first," he said, his eyes tenderly meeting mine. "Meanwhile, we've got two fine little ornaments to start your tradition off with."

I burst out laughing and he did too. "All right," I said. "I'll go get some things from the store." I sat up straight and braced my hand on his chest. "But I won't be able to buy enough to fill that tree unless you want me to rob a bank first."

Jackson's hands cupped my face. "No," he said. "I have some other ideas before you go robbing banks . . ."

❄

Christmas Season 2018

I stared at the photo of Sara that Jackson had taken during her first Christmas, our second. He'd had a Things Remembered gift store in Savannah make into an ornament for our third Christmas. Our cherry-cheeked angel, sitting up as best she could with her gifts around her. In the background, the barely decorated Fraser fir dwarfed her, as it had everything else in the room. Its size had stressed me then, but from the moment I'd pulled the silver, engraved ornament from the toe of my stocking, it only brought smiles and laughter wrapped in its memory.

Having taken it out of its box, I found just the right branch for it, hung it, and stood back to take in the few ornaments I'd hung against the whole of the tree. I then reached into the bin and pulled out the ornament Jackson had given me the year Travis had made his entry into the world on Christmas Day.

We'd returned home from the hospital on December 27 with Travis cradled in my arms. Mrs. Morgan waited for us at the house with Sara, and Dad arrived a short time later so we could have our official Christmas and open gifts. Somehow, Jackson had managed to find time to drive to Statesboro and purchase a crescent-shaped moon ornament with a blue bear sleeping in its curve and have Travis's full name and date of birth engraved on it. A star dangled from the tip of the moon and, fourteen years later, I used my fingertip to make it dance.

❄

December 27, 2004

After all the gifts had been opened and the wrapping paper wadded up and stuffed into the large kitchen trashcan, Dad found me in the nursery, changing my son's diaper and cooing to him as he stared up at me.

"You doing okay?" he asked, putting his hand on my shoulder and peering over to get a good look at his first grandson. "Hey there, little fella," he said to Travis, who blinked in return.

"I'm a tad tired," I told him truthfully. "Nothing about this pregnancy was easy, so it seems like nine months of hard labor instead of only a few hours."

Dad kissed the side of my head near my temple. "Try to get some rest tonight, huh?"

I didn't answer. I now had a busy five-year-old and an infant. Would I ever sleep again? "I feel—" I began, but then stopped myself.

"What?"

I shook my head as I pulled Travis's little UGA sweatpants over his diaper and then scooped him up and brought him to my shoulder.

"Talk to me, sweetheart," Dad coaxed.

I turned to look at him fully. "Dad," I said, trying to keep the tears that threatened to spill over any second at bay. "Do you think— will I ever—do you think I'll ever get *my* life back?" I shook my head again. "That didn't come out like I meant it."

Dad gathered me and my son in his arms as he shushed me. "I know what you meant."

"Do you?" I buried my face into his neck and breathed in the familiar scent of my father, safe in its security. "I love my children, Daddy, but I'm getting a sense that I may never—"

Dad held me at arm's length. "Listen to me, now. Some of this is hormones and some of this is an old dream that has been buried."

"Twice."

"Leesha, I've told you this your whole life, but let me say it one more time. You make your own happy, little girl. You can see this as some sort of punishment or postponement or whatever, but look around you. Jackson turned out all right."

"Yes."

"There's no doubt in my mind that he loves you. Whatever mistakes the two of you made before you got married—"

"Mistake, Dad. Once."

"Doesn't matter."

"I just don't want you to think—"

"*It doesn't matter, Leesha.* You're missing the point. You've got to find your happiness, my girl. Because it's right here." He extended both arms, palms up. "All you have to do is let go and enjoy it."

I nodded as I pressed my lips to my son's head. "Okay. I hear you." I smiled.

"What's the smile for?"

"I was just thinking . . . a minute ago I smelled your cologne and how it mixes with, you know, *you*. And just now I caught that wonderful scent of a newborn and . . . one day, this will be gone and he'll smell more like . . . you."

"Well, first you have to get through that little-boy-sweat stage."

I laughed easily.

"See there?" Dad said. "You're already finding your own happy."

CHAPTER TWELVE

January 2005

I decided January 1—a resolution of sorts—that I *would* find my own happy. I doted on my children and on Jackson by creating the happiest home I knew how.

Monday through Friday, Jackson and I rose early, had our coffee and breakfast together in the tiny dining room, where I'd painted the walls a warm shade of melon trimmed in creamy white. Then, as he got ready for work in our bathroom, I roused Sara from her slumber by scooping her in my arms and carrying her into the dining room, while planting tiny kisses all over her face as she groaned, "Oh, Mommy . . . five more minutes, please."

Placing her in her chair, I'd say, "Eat your cereal. If you get ready in time, I'll let you watch a cartoon before you leave for school."

By the time Jackson swept out of our bedroom smelling of soap and aftershave and looking too handsome for his own good, I had dressed Sara, helped get her teeth brushed, and placed her little backpack by the front door. Jackson usually found me in the nursery, kissed me and our son goodbye, and then went into the living room to spend time with Sara before leaving for the day.

I kept our home immaculate. Our children, folks said, looked as if I'd "dressed them and then pressed them." After our morning routine, I often drove up to Morgan's around noon to take Jackson his lunch and to allow him a little time with Travis. In the afternoons, before Sara returned from school, I busied myself with meal preparations, then dashed out to pick her up.

Evenings were spent as a family. Jackson took over with bedtime rituals while I washed and dried the dishes, making sure the kitchen was tidy before heading to bed myself.

Five days a week we did this. On Saturday Jackson tiptoed around, letting me and the children sleep in a little later than usual, and on Sunday we flew around in a frenzy to get ourselves to church followed by lunch at either Dad's or Mrs. Morgan's.

And we remained at this pace through the next three years as Sara grew into a precocious darling and Travis ran at breakneck speed around the house, talking nonstop and giggling at anything that moved. And I thought I couldn't be happier.

Or that Jackson couldn't be happier.

But happiness can also be an illusion, and a strange thing happens when a man stops reaching for his wife at night. She doesn't always notice at first, but—with enough time—she begins to wonder. Her mind begins to stray and question and, eventually, become frantic, and all at the same time.

Add to that the moodiness, the one-line answers to questions that deserved more, and the late work hours, and I felt like the greatest fool on the planet.

That I had somehow been sucker-punched by the love fairy.

But I had a plan. Jackson Morgan wasn't going to up and leave me defenseless with two small children. Not me. I'd heard stories such as these, but I wouldn't play the lead role in some tragic Lifetime movie. No, no. I had a plan.

"I want to go back to school," I repeated the line I'd spoken years before. The day had slipped into late evening. The children and I had eaten, I'd gotten them ready for bed, tucked them in, and read each a book before listening to bedtime prayers and calling for shut-eye. Jackson walked through the front door not ten minutes later holding a manila folder stuffed with papers and a bone-weary expression on his face.

He looked like all he wanted was a shower and a hot meal, but I planted my feet, crossed my arms, and said the rehearsed words before he could even say hello.

My husband blinked at me. "What?"

"You heard me."

He walked from the living room and into the dining room in three strides, throwing the folder on the table as he passed through on his way to the kitchen. "Leesha, now is not the time."

I followed behind to find him standing before an open refrigerator, pulling the gallon-sized Rubbermaid pitcher of iced tea from the top shelf. "Jackson, I want to go back to school."

I'm not sure what I expected, but his slamming the pitcher on the counter before pushing past me on his way to our bedroom wasn't it. "Kids asleep?" he asked over his shoulder.

"Jackson, please. Listen to me."

I entered the room as he shrugged out of his Morgan's tee, back muscles rippling in a way that distracted me even when I didn't want them to. He placed his hands on his hips, fingers spread wide, and breathed out of his nostrils like a bull about to charge. "Is that what you want?" He dropped the shirt on the bed without turning to face me.

"Yes. Don't you think I deserve to go back?"

He nodded. "If that's what you want, Leesha, go ahead. But my kids are not going to suffer for it."

I crossed the room and snatched up the shirt. "Your kids? *Your* kids?"

His eyes flashed anger and then, within a modicum of a second, became apologetic. "Our kids. You know what I mean."

"I would never neglect our children."

He breathed out again. "Whatever you want to do, Leesha. Just—" He looked toward the door. "Did you save me anything for dinner?"

"Don't I always?"

"Yeah." He unbuckled his belt to finish undressing. "I'm going to get a shower, okay?"

I diverted my eyes. "Okay," I answered quietly. "I'll have your supper ready for you when you get out."

I found Jackson later that night, pen in hand, poring over the file at the dining room table. His dinner plate had been pushed toward the middle of the table, its contents only half eaten. "Are you done?" I asked softly.

He glanced up. "Yeah."

I took the plate, aware of the chill in the room and the chasm between us. Problem was, I couldn't figure out where it had originated. Or why it had so engulfed us. After rinsing the plate and placing it in the dishwasher, I turned off the kitchen light and stepped toward our bedroom, hoping not to disturb Jackson from whatever had his attention. But I heard him call my name as I flipped on our bedroom light. Gently. Coaxing me to come to where he sat.

Even though unsure as to whether to pretend I'd not heard him or to return to the dining room, I chose the latter. I stood in the doorway between the dining room and kitchen and leaned against the frame, crossing my ankles and folding my hands together. Jackson remained in his chair, forearms pressed against the table's edge, the papers from the folder spread out around him. A pen in one hand, poised over a legal pad, shook slightly between his fingers. The expression on my husband's face showed fear and anger, concern and determination. "Can you sit for a minute?"

I pulled the chair directly across from him out from the table and sat, saying nothing. Waiting.

Jackson sighed. "I think someone is stealing from the store."

My shoulders sagged from the weight of his words. "What? Are you sure?"

"We've been losing money for the past few months and none of it makes sense. I've gone over these books time and again. I've watched everyone. I've installed cameras. I don't—I can't even begin to imagine any of my guys doing this."

This explained so much. Not another woman . . . not a heart thief at all. I leaned over, stretching my hand toward his, which he gave freely. "How much is missing?"

"Enough to keep me awake at night. Enough to put us in serious danger if I don't figure this out sooner rather than later." His brow furrowed. "Listen, Leesha . . . about earlier."

"It's okay. I get it now."

"No. No, you don't. I know you want to go back to school. I do. But right now . . . until I figure this out, we just can't afford it."

"It's okay."

"It's not okay. I've done this to you three times now." He hung his head and squeezed his eyes closed. "I'm sorry, Leesha. I really am."

CHAPTER THIRTEEN

Christmas Season 2018

I bent to remove another wrapped ornament from the bin, pulling the tissue paper away carefully, followed by the square sheet of bubble wrap that gave final protection to an ornament that never failed to stir the oddest of emotions. The first, a deep sick feeling that rolled around in the pit of my stomach, a dark memory that tries to stay buried but then must, if only for a moment, raise its head until another memory comes along to shove it down.

I laid my fingertips over the heart-shaped ornament and closed my eyes, willing the second emotion to be strong enough to do exactly that.

❄

2008

Within a few weeks, Jackson uncovered the truth. His father's longtime employee Neil Dean had developed a drug habit and had fed that habit with the store's money. But by then, Morgan's had fallen into serious financial trouble. Jackson was forced to let some of his part-time employees go "until things get better," which meant him working longer, harder hours. Mrs. Morgan volunteered to watch Travis three days a week, which allowed me enough free time to work at the store as well.

If I had hoped the revelations and what went with them would aid in my relationship with Jackson, I was sadly mistaken. Between long store hours came the investigations, court hearings, and depositions. Worse still was the knowledge that someone Jackson had looked up to as a father figure had betrayed his trust.

By the first part of December 2008, as exhaustion threatened every fiber of my body, and Jackson seemed to have pulled further away than before, I found myself wondering if our marriage would survive what scant bit was left of the year. "Perhaps our *next* court appearance will be in front of a divorce attorney," I told Callie as we moved along one aisle of Washburn's Department Store. She pushed her twins' stroller in front of us.

Callie grabbed my forearm. "Don't even tease about a thing like that."

But I wasn't teasing. Every morning and every evening and often several times a day, I asked God for the strength to see our marriage through this circumstance. Yet, every day, as Christmas music filled stores and car radios, and even as we decorated for the holiday and folks called out, "Merry Christmas," my heart grew harder and Jackson's grew quieter. The only ones he doted on were Sara and Travis. They had his full-on attention, the store has his full-on attention, and I was left with less than the dregs.

And then . . . December 18, 2008. A Tuesday, and a frigid one at that. The temperature had dropped to a 101-year low, bringing promises of a rare white Christmas. Sara ran around the house singing "I'm dreaming of a . . ." with Travis skipping behind her, when the house phone rang.

I answered to hear Jackson's trembling voice on the other end, his words broken by gulps of fear. "Mom's been in an accident . . . car spun out of control . . . it's pretty bad, Leesh . . . heading up to the hospital now."

My heart froze. "I'll get Callie to watch the kids and meet you there."

"No," he said. "You don't need to come. I've got this."

"Jackson. Stop forcing me out. You don't have to go this alone—"

"I wasn't trying to go it alone, Felicia. I just don't need—"

"I'm coming up there, Jackson," I forced out. Deep down, what I really wanted was to give him what he wanted, to leave him alone to wallow in his own self-made misery. But I knew I couldn't.

If anything happened to his mother . . .

Thoughts of the night I'd gone to him after hearing that his father had died rushed in. Thoughts rushed over me of how I'd stretched out beside him on the twin bed at the far end of the room. Of how—in his grief over losing his father and my renewed grief over losing my mother—we'd held on too tightly and kissed too fervently . . . and in the process made a baby. Old guilt met new fear.

But I was no longer that nineteen-year-old girl. Jackson was no longer some boy I dated in high school. He was my husband. The father of my children. "I'm calling Callie," I said again before ending the call.

I found Jackson in the emergency room waiting area still wearing his heaviest winter jacket, his Morgan's baseball cap pulled low over his forehead, his gloves gripped in both hands as though they were a lifeline, and his elbows resting on his knees. His eyes were closed, and his lips moved in a silent prayer as his feet bobbed up and down as though they couldn't be still.

I took the seat beside him, slid my arm along his shoulder, and waited for him to look at me. When he did, I saw the streaks of tears, the wet eyelashes . . . so much like the time before. And, like the time before, I held out my arms and gathered him into an embrace meant only to comfort. Or to bring strength. "Jackson," I breathed out. "I'm here."

"I'm so sorry," he spoke into the curve of my neck. "I'm so sorry. I think God is punishing me for being—I'm so sorry . . ."

"God is doing no such thing," I reassured him. "God doesn't work like that."

He pulled back, and I dug into my purse for the travel-size tissues I'd learned to keep with me at all times, especially with little children in tow. "Here," I said, handing him one. "Now, tell me. What are the doctors saying? Is she—"

He wiped his nose and shook his head. "She's pretty bad off, Leesh. No promises, of course, but they think she should make it." He nodded then. "But the next few days are going to be critical and, if she does pull through, it's going to be a slow recovery . . ."

I had learned all things worthwhile are.

We spent the entire holiday at the hospital. I hired a neighbor's teenage daughter to watch the children during Christmas break, which allowed me to be at the hospital during the day while Jackson worked, and then, a short while after Jackson entered his mother's room, I returned home to two wired children. Now, instead of wondering if our marriage would survive, I wondered if my mother-in-law would.

Christmas Day arrived as it always did, and yet, in spite of the stress, Jackson kept to tradition. I couldn't imagine what ornament he might have purchased to commemorate the year. I didn't know whether to laugh or cry when I found a Bakersville General Hospital ornament in my stocking, but one look at Jackson's face told me he required nothing but a smile.

"We'll never forget this one, will we?" he grinned.

"I should say not."

And then he drew me into his arms and kissed me, right in front of the children. "I love you," he said.

I glanced over at Sara, who beamed with all the imagination of a nine-year-old, then back to her father's waiting face. "I love you too," I told him.

Shortly before New Year's Day, we had received the news that while Jackson's mother would make a full recovery in time, she would first need rehab followed by months of continual in-home care. Jackson and I, along with his siblings and their spouses—all who lived out of town—agreed that the best call to action was for our small family to move into Jackson's childhood home.

Had we had more time, perhaps, we would have chosen another route. But our decision seemed right at the moment. We packed our clothes and personal belongings into large suitcases and a few boxes and headed to the Morgan family home.

By the time Mrs. Morgan returned to the house with her temporary walker, Jackson and I had slept in the guest bedroom for nearly a week, Sara had taken Jackson's sister's old bedroom, and Travis had all his toys unpacked in the room his father had shared with his brother Terrance.

By the following Christmas, Jackson had dubbed our time at Mrs. Morgan's as "the craziest of our lives." We could kid about it later on, but while it was happening it wasn't so funny. Mrs. Morgan was a demanding patient, and I was a nurse one nerve short on patience. Not that I ever let *her* know it, but I didn't hold back when it came to Jackson, who endured my gripes and complaints with a tight jaw and hard eyes.

We sold our lovely Craftsman because—as Mrs. Morgan insisted—it no longer made sense to pay mortgage on a place no one lived in. And, amazingly, we got twice what we'd initially paid for it. The business turned around, bringing in a substantial profit. So much so, Jackson came up with an idea to open up other branches in nearby towns, which—to my way of thinking—meant he'd be at work even more often and with me even less. I didn't know whether to be grateful or angry.

Finally, in a rare moment of comradery, we agreed that the time to move out of Mrs. Morgan's was nearing. We put a down payment on a rambling Victorian located on the outskirts of town in an area of Bakersville where old money had—once upon a time—used their new money to build such places, and which up-and-comers now purchased. Exactly one year from the date of the accident, Jackson and I moved out of Mrs. Morgan's and turned the key in the rattling double doors of our new home for the first time. "Merry Christmas," Jackson said as he ceremoniously scooped me into his arms and carried me over the threshold. "And happy anniversary . . ." He kissed me soundly. Something he hadn't done for quite a while. "For about the next thirty years."

And for the first time in a long time, we laughed.

Not that the good humor would last. My stocking held an engraved silver "best nurse" ornament that boasted a sparkling Swarovski crystal within a stethoscope that wove itself into the shape of a heart. I thanked him, and I meant it. But with all that had happened in the past two years, I wondered . . . if I were able to use that stethoscope . . . if I were able to put it against my own chest . . . would my heart still beat there?

Or had it grown too apathetic to try?

CHAPTER FOURTEEN

Christmas Season 2018

I found the perfect branch for what Jackson ended up calling the Nurse Leesha ornament. "Or maybe," he said, "we should call it Nurse Ratched."

"Cute. That's what you are."

"Best you became a fulltime mother than a fulltime nurse," he had quipped.

Which only served to remind me that I had not wanted to be a fulltime mother. I had wanted something more, although I sure couldn't put my finger on it now. Nor, were I completely honest, had I ever really been able to. One day my children would walk out the front door and into their own lives. One day, I would be alone—although with a seven-year-old I had more of a wait than I'd anticipated before his arrival.

Had I driven Jackson away? Had my inability to get past our issues caused me to shut him out in the same way he had shut me out a decade before? If I had been a little more open about my fears once Monica Craig returned to town . . . if I'd given her less credit than she deserved when it came to the disintegration of my marriage, maybe Jackson wouldn't have left. Should I have fought harder? Would it have made a difference?

And what about now? Was there hope? Even if Jackson now shared some sort of a relationship with Monica, the most important thing for our children was—

Lumbering footsteps descended the staircase, startling me. I looked over my shoulder to see Hank, lips broad with a smile and eyes aglow. "Daddy's here with Trav," he said, heading for the front door.

"Hank, your coat—" I began, but once again my words were cut short by the slamming of the door.

I went to the foyer hall bench and coat tree to retrieve mine. Within a moment, Travis opened the door, letting in a blast of cold air. "Hey, Mom." He pulled a wool cap from his head, which sent his straight blond hair in all directions.

I slid my arms into my coat sleeves. "Hey, yourself. Good day?"

"Pretty good. Where are you going?"

I plastered on a smile. "I just need to tell your dad something."

His face went blank. "Y'all aren't going to fight again, are you?"

Squeezing his lips together between my pressing fingers, I teased, "No-we-aren't-going-to-fight-again." Releasing his face, I added, "We've done more than fight over the years, you know. How do you think *you* got here?"

Mock horror crossed his face. "*Eww, Mom*, don't even joke about things like that." He overexaggerated the willies as he shrugged out of his coat.

I laughed easily on my way out the door. Hank was halfway up the steps as Jackson watched him from his truck. He'd already opened the driver's door and had one foot perched on the running board. Seeing me, he jutted his chin upward and said, "Hey."

"Hold on," I told him. "I need to tell you something."

Hank looked up at me with the same look Travis had given me moments before, wondering if Mommy and Daddy were going to fight again. "Go on inside," I told him quietly. "It's okay."

The front door closed behind me as Jackson shut his truck's to keep the heat inside, then took his familiar pose—feet braced apart, arms folded. Refusing to be challenged. I rubbed my hands together to fight off the cold and smiled. "Hey," I said, stopping close enough to him to keep our conversation between the two of us, but far enough away not to appear intimate. "I just wanted you to know that Christmas Eve is fine with me. You're right. We don't have years to alternate with family anymore."

Jackson's brow shot up. "I'm *what*?"

I gave him my best aren't-you-cute look. "Very funny."

He relaxed and leaned against the truck's door, crossing his legs at the ankles. "No, no," he teased. "Say that again. Because I'm sure I didn't hear you the first time." He leaned his ear toward me in mock deafness. "I'm what?"

I frowned. "You were right," I said slowly. "There now. Are you happy?"

Seriousness relaxed his smile. "Not entirely, but that'll do for a start."

I fought back a grin as he opened the truck and got in, but I watched as he backed out of the drive, which I had not done in a long time. I wasn't sure what came over me, except that something in the playfulness Jackson and I had exchanged resonated an old emotion I'd thought long ago buried. It had warmed me. Made me smile several times as I prepared dinner and again as I put Hank to bed and said goodnight to Travis.

After my shower and after crawling into my lonely bed, I wrestled with the entire notion that had come to me as I held my phone and stared at the face of it. Should I call him? And, if I did, what would we talk about? And, what if he was with Monica? Would that anger him? My disruption of their date?

Even more . . . how would she react at this reminder that Jackson Morgan was still married?

I smiled at the thought, then called him.

Jackson answered almost immediately. "What's wrong?" Sleep clouded his voice.

"Nothing, why? Did I wake you?"

"Yeah, but that's okay." But he groaned just the same.

"I didn't realize how late—"

"No, no. It's okay. Are you sure something's not wrong?"

I threw my hand up in the air as though waving off a silly notion. "No. The boys are in bed and I—well, I was thinking about Christmas—"

"You said you were okay with Christmas Eve, remember?" He sighed a sort of moan, and I pictured him pushing himself up in bed, the linens falling around his waist, his upper body sporting a long-sleeved tee as it always did in the colder months.

But in the warmer months, he wore no shirt at all . . .

"I know. I said you were right." I chuckled lightly. "I spent all of dinner trying not to choke on my food as it worked itself past the knot."

He laughed then, low and throaty.

"I actually called to talk to you about Christmas gifts."

"You don't have to buy me anything."

I leaned against the stack of pillows behind me and smiled. "Not you and me, doofus. The children. I thought maybe we should meet up. Maybe for lunch? Talk about what we're getting them so we don't duplicate?"

A pause met my suggestion, and my breath caught until he said, "Our stores have been crazy busy lately. I haven't been able to eat so much as a packet of peanut butter crackers for lunch in weeks."

"Oh. I see."

"But how about dinner some night? Sara will be back when? Saturday?"

"Saturday by noon. Or, at least that's what she said last time we talked about it."

"Yeah. That's what she told me too. I didn't schedule her until next week."

"She said she and *Billy* are going out for their Christmas celebration before he heads home to Charlotte for the holidays."

"Leesha," Jackson said slowly. "He's a good kid. And *she's* a good kid. Don't worry so much."

"I know, I know. They're not us." I squeezed my eyes shut in regret at my choice of words.

"We weren't so bad," Jackson spoke into the quiet.

"That's what scares me, Jackson."

He didn't answer, leaving me to wonder where his thoughts had gone. Then, "So, how about dinner Friday night? Work for you?"

Friday night. I grinned all over myself. Well, at least he didn't have plans with Monica. "What time?"

"Seven?"

"Sounds good. Where should I meet you?"

"Don't be silly, Leesha. I'll pick you up. Nothing fancy, though. Wear jeans." I started to comment further but his next words interrupted me. "And that pink sweater. I always liked you in that pink sweater."

I bit down hard on my lower lip, knowing full well my face had completely flushed.

Chapter Fifteen

"That pink sweater?" Treva asked with a grin as we stirred creamer into our coffees. She leaned against the counter in the break room. "Well, now . . . I *do* like the sound of that."

"Don't get carried away. We're only going to meet to talk about the children and their Christmas gifts." I took a tentative sip of the steaming drink. "And I'll probably wear that cream-colored sweater with the gold thread." I walked toward the door as she placed her spoon next to mine in the sink.

"The off-shoulder one?"

I frowned at her as we stepped from the break room and into the hallway. "It can be worn *on* the shoulder as well."

She wiggled her brow. "But you *can* wear it off the shoulder."

"Treva." I turned toward my office as she headed toward hers. "Don't create something that's not there," I said over my shoulder.

"It's there all right," she finished with a laugh.

I shook my head at her but couldn't help whispering a prayer, thanking God for bringing her into my life.

❄

October 2010

"Mom!" Eleven-year-old Sara barreled into the rambling Victorian. "Mommy, wait till you hear!"

"I'm in the kitchen," I called to her and, when she came in red-cheeked from the late October chill, I added, "How was school? Obviously exciting."

"Mom, wait till you hear." She dropped her backpack on the floor before pulling her lightweight jacket off, then bent to retrieve something out of the backpack. "My new best friend Tiffany has invited me to join Holy Hands with her." Sara whipped out a flyer made on green construction paper and handed it to me.

"What is Holy Hands?" I asked, even as I read the information.

"They use sign language to interpret songs. Hymns and stuff like that." She pointed to the exact same wording on the paper. "Tiff said even though I don't go to her church, I can join. Can I, Mom?"

"And Tiffany's the girl you've been talking to on the phone till all hours lately?"

"Yes, ma'am. She and I have *so* much in common. She's truly my best friend now. So, can I?"

I couldn't see any reason why not. "And they meet when?" I looked for the time and place.

"Every Wednesday!" She jumped up and down. "That's tonight. Will you take me?"

I smiled at my daughter. "You're really excited about this, aren't you?"

"They're having a Christmas show, and Tiff said I'm getting in just in time. After this week, I can't join *and* be in the program."

"All right then," I said, setting the paper on the old farmhouse table I'd recently restored. "Let's you and Travis and me have an early supper, and then I'll take you."

Treva Hicks met me early that evening with a firm handshake and a wider-than-life smile when Sara, Travis, and I entered the youth wing of the church Tiffany and her family attended. "Tiffany has already told me all about you, Sara. She's so excited you're joining us. Why don't you go sit over there next to her, and I'll talk to your mom a minute."

Sara dashed off toward a pretty girl with long dark hair and a face full of freckles and an equally as infectious smile as my daughter sported at that moment while Treva leaned over to ask Travis his name and whether or not he was interested in joining. "No, thank you," he told her. "I'll just watch."

I placed my hand on Travis's shoulder. "Now if you had offered to toss a football or a baseball in all this sign language, he's your man."

Treva laughed. "Stick around if you'd like," she said. "You know, if you'd like to see what we do."

"I'd like that," I told her, then guided Travis to a row of folding chairs where, for the next forty-five minutes, we watched Treva conduct sign language instruction. I couldn't take my eyes away from her. She reminded me more of my mother than anyone I'd met since Mom's death. Not so much in looks—Treva's skin a honey-black and Mom's more peaches and cream—but more in the way she interacted with the children, the way her styled hair shimmered under the lights, the way she laughed when one of the children messed up instead of reprimanding them.

My mother had been like that. Never a reprimand. But then again, I'd never really done anything to disappoint her. I'd left that for *after* her death. I'd left that for Dad to deal with alone.

Treva and I exchanged phone numbers that evening and, the next day, she called and invited me to a ladies Bible study held at her home on Monday nights. I explained that I'd have to clear it with my husband—that he often worked later than the actual store hours—but that I'd get back to her soon.

As it turned out, Jackson seemed pleased that I wanted to join the study. "You give so much to me and the kids," he said matter-of-factly. "You deserve a little time away from the house and all. A little you and God time."

I didn't know whether to feel complimented or insulted.

On the first Monday night, after the seven or eight women of the group shared a little about themselves with me—where they worked, how long they'd been married, the number of children they had, and where they attended church—I did the same. "I'm a fulltime wife and mother," I said, "Although now that both of my children are in school, I'm hoping that I can either go to work or, perhaps—maybe—go back to school . . ." The last four words trailed on a broken dream and two unexpected pregnancies.

After the group dismissed, Treva asked me to stay a moment longer. "There's a job opening at the law office I work in, if you are interested."

"A law office?" A light chuckle escaped my lungs. "Did I hear you correctly? A law office?"

Treva laughed with me, even though my joy was lost on her. "Langford, Hancock and Associates," she said. "We need a file clerk. It's a simple job, but if you take to it, you could be trained later as a legal secretary or perhaps even one of the boys' research clerks."

"The boys?"

She laughed. "That's what I call the attorneys." She winked. "Keeps them in their place."

I grinned all over myself as I mulled over the prospects of the job, which sounded interesting. "What do I need to do?" I asked as we headed for her front door.

"Just come by the office tomorrow. I'm the office manager, so ask for me. This will be the easiest first interview you ever had."

Over the next few weeks, Jackson and I managed to keep life at status quo, which was pretty much as we'd done since moving into the house. When I initially told Jackson about the job offer, he reminded me that I didn't *have* to work. That he made enough money for the both of us and he didn't want the kids to suffer by me not having enough time for them.

We stood on opposite sides of our bed, tossing throw pillows to the floor and pulling back the comforter. "But if I can find someone to watch them for the hour and a half between them getting out of school and me getting home, would that be all right?" The notion that I had to practically beg my husband for permission to work riled me, though I managed to keep my frustrations at bay. A practice I'd grown good at over the years.

"Jackson," I continued, "it's either that I'm taking the job as the file clerk or I'm going back to school. I always said I would as soon as Travis entered first grade, and I'm already a semester behind. Obviously, at this point I can't get in until next year, but—I was thinking—Treva mentioned a research clerk's position. You know. Maybe. One day." I climbed onto the four-poster rice bed—in all our years of marriage, the first bed we'd owned *truly* big enough for Jackson's frame—and settled between the cold sheets, then adjusted the blanket. "So I'm thinking that for now, I'll take the file clerk position and then . . . maybe, one day, when it comes available . . . I can move up to a research clerk. I've always liked research, and it has *some* connections with my studies at Southern."

Jackson got into bed beside me, smelling of soap and peppermint toothpaste. He slipped his watch off and laid it on the bedside table next to him. "All right, Leesh. If that's what you want." He sighed as he dropped his head onto the pillows. "I'm bushed. How about you?"

I sank down and turned my back to him, waiting for him to spoon with me. A second later, his arm came around me, and I snuggled in. "You're always bushed."

"Things are hopping at the store," he said, then kissed the back of my head. "Night, Leesha."

I reached for the bedside lamp and twisted the switch. "Night, Jackson."

CHAPTER SIXTEEN

December 2010

"I think we should change our anniversary date or Travis's birthday," Jackson said from the breakfast table one Sunday in early December as he pored over the monthly calendar filled with scheduled events.

Travis's head popped up from over his cereal bowl. "Huh?"

Jackson laughed at our son, then tossed his hair. "I'm joshing with you." Then he looked up at me. "I'm serious, though. Look at this. School parties. Church events. Our anniversary—"

"Which we never celebrate," I interjected from the counter we used as a coffee station.

Jackson puckered his lips and dramatically kissed the air. "Every day is a celebration with you, Leesh."

Sara diverted her attention from the book she was reading long enough to say, "Aww," to which Travis added his "Eww."

"Leesha, what's this thing here? S's HHP."

I finished pouring coffee into Jackson's favorite mug and brought it to where he sat, then peered over his shoulder. "That's Sara's Holy Hands performance."

Sara kept her nose pointed toward the book, but managed to say, "Y'all are gonna love it."

"Is that the thing you've been going to on Wednesday nights?"

Now Sara looked up, her eyes dancing. "Daddy, wait till you see. Tiffany and me are doing—"

"Tiffany and I," I corrected her as I took my own place at the table.

She groaned. "Tiffany and *I* are doing a special number. Have you ever heard Amy Grant's 'Breath of Heaven'?"

Jackson shook his head while I nodded.

"Oh, good," Sara said, then closed her book to concentrate on her Cheerios. "That's at least one of my parents. You're going to be so proud when you see *I* do this." She crossed her eyes at me, and I shook my head at her, all the while wondering *which* parent she spoke of. Was she glad I *had* heard the song or that Jackson had *not*?

Either way, Sara was correct. Jackson and I were both extremely proud of her, although for a while there, I thought I'd be the only one to see her performance. The only one to cheer her on afterward.

As usual, Jackson worked late that night. And as usual, I got both kids ready by myself while the clock ticked louder by the second with Sara moaning over it—"I *have* to be there early, Mom. I can't be late,"—as though the world would come to an absolute end should she be five minutes behind schedule.

"I'll get you there," I told her, my voice filled with exasperation. "I'm on my own here, you know," I added between gritted teeth as I jammed my feet into the boots I'd left by the hallway bench and coat tree. "Okay, let's go! What are we waiting on?"

True to form, in Jackson's superhero sort of way, as the Holy Hands choir walked out from the wings and onto the stage, my husband slipped into the empty seat beside me. He'd somehow managed to get home, shower, change, and look so incredibly handsome and well put together, I almost forgot to be angry with him.

Almost.

Travis immediately left his seat to crawl into his father's lap. "Travis," I whispered. "You're too big for this."

"I can't see over that lady's big head," he whispered back, although a little louder than I would have preferred.

I cringed as the woman sporting over-teased hair in the row in front of us turned, looked at me, and frowned. One sideward glance at Jackson told me all I needed to know. While our son's words had mortified his mother, his father bit back laughter.

Halfway through the program, Tiffany and Sara stepped away from the rest of the choir to perform the sign language interpretation of a song lifted from Mary's heart to her heavenly Father. Pleading through the unknown of what lay ahead, she expressed haunting words of both fear and faith.

As my daughter's hands glided through the air and her face expressed the lyrics, I pressed my lips together, remembering. I *knew* that fear. I'd prayed that prayer. And now, the result of a single moment's lack of judgment stood so eloquent and graceful, sharing an oft-forgotten piece of the gospel with a room full of spectators. They, like Jackson and me, sat raptured. I could feel the collective catch of breath, the exuding of awe, all around us.

My own tears came too easily, blurring the stage, the choir, and the two young girls who stood in its center. I blinked and they escaped, trailing down my cheeks and running the length of my jawline. And then, as if on cue, Jackson's hand found mine. My eyes found his. And I knew.

He and I had thought the same thing.

That night in the privacy of our bedroom, overcome by emotion at the performance, awed by the love and pride I felt for our daughter, and blanketed by an unbreakable bond with my husband, I found myself reaching for him in a way I'd never done before. And Jackson . . . Jackson found himself completely lost in the moment as well, startled by whatever the night had unleashed in me. The next morning, between the snuggles and kisses, he told me once again that he wanted to do better. Be more present. Become a better husband.

"You're a wonderful husband," I told him, then kissed his jaw.

"But I want to be better," he said. "And with God's help, Leesha, I will."

Christmas morning that year, my stocking boasted an exquisite sterling silver ornament, its relief depicting Mary and Joseph heading toward Bethlehem—Joseph leading the way, one hand holding a staff, the other holding the reins of the donkey Mary sat upon. Her hand rested atop a round belly and her face looked onward . . . outward . . . into the great unknown where God led and needed her to be.

I knew Jackson had purchased the ornament in remembrance of our daughter's performance and of our night together afterward. But this ornament became more than a remembrance. This one became a prophetic gift.

Nine months later, I again held a newborn in my arms and fell crazy in love for the third time.

Chapter Seventeen

Christmas Season 2018

Jackson's truck pulled into the driveway at precisely seven o'clock.

Travis hollered up the staircase to let me know "Dad's here." But when I didn't come down from my bedroom right away, he bounded up the stairs and knocked on the door. "Mom? Did you hear me?"

I opened it slowly, then smiled. "Now isn't that better than bellowing like a fish wife?"

But if Travis was meant to feel the sting of my rebuke, he didn't. Instead he stepped back and whistled. "Wow, Mom. Did you get a new sweater or something?"

I turned once, showing off the shapely Christmas-red, calf-length cardigan I'd purchased on sale the previous year at Vanessa's. "Not new. I've just not worn it yet."

"Well, you look . . . well, hot." His eyes grew buggy and he added, "I can't believe I just said that about my own mother."

I walked past him as the front doorbell rang. "Now, listen. Make sure Hank doesn't eat too much junk while I'm out."

"I won't," he said, trailing behind me.

Hank tore out of his room about that time, heading for the stairs, but Travis caught him near the landing. "Woah, there . . . not tonight."

"But—" Hank protested.

"Not tonight, sport. Ya gotta go with me on this one."

I winked at my older son. "Thanks, Trav."

"Yeah, well," he said standing. "Don't do anything I'm too young to do."

I shook my head and continued down the stairs as Hank asked his brother, "Like what? What are you too young to do?"

When I opened the door, Jackson smiled warmly. "It's not pink, but it looks nice," he said. "Very Christmassy."

"Thank you," choosing not to reveal just how many tops I'd tried on before settling on this one. I reached for my scarf and coat hanging on the hall bench and coat tree. "You look nice yourself."

And he did. He wore an untucked port-colored oxford shirt whose tails trailed beneath the hem of an ecru rollneck fisherman's sweater. His jeans looked new and I wondered if he'd bought them for our date.

Not that this was a date. This was just two parents getting together to discuss their children's Christmas lists. But I allowed him to place his hand on the small of my back as we walked to the passenger's side of the truck and to open the door for me. And I allowed a warmth to move through me as he started the engine, looked across the seat at me, and said, "You really do look pretty tonight, Leesh."

Just two parents, I reminded myself again, even as I said, "And you look handsome too, Jackson." Not that I could ever think of a time when he didn't. Even at his worst, Jackson had a look that managed to weaken my knees and bring a warmth to my heart. I could be angry. I could be downright furious with him at times. But I could never deny the way one look at him made me feel.

Jackson took me to a small barbecue restaurant, one we'd been to more times than I could count and one we both enjoyed. We saw a few of our friends who gave us a double take, but Jackson strolled by each table, shaking the hands of the men and giving a polite "Merry Christmas" to the women.

Blessedly, the hostess led us to a back corner booth and, for a crazy moment, I wondered if Jackson had called ahead and reserved the private, more intimate, space. But, like pixie dust that falls lovely then lands on the earth with nothing much left to give, he said, "What luck, huh?"

"Meaning?" I asked, sliding onto the bench seat.

Jackson took the seat opposite from mine. "Getting this booth. That way we can talk uninterrupted." Then he laughed lightly as his eyes scanned the restaurant. "I think we're going to have the gossips talking nonstop tomorrow."

I rolled my eyes. "What's new with that?"

After the waitress came and took our order, Jackson got right down to business. "So, tell me what you're thinking for Christmas. Have the kids mentioned anything to you about what they're hoping for?"

"Sara loves those Ginger Snaps necklaces, so I went to Vanessa's the other day and bought her a new one plus about five more snaps." I paused, waiting. Wondering if he would mention Monica Craig. Praying he wouldn't say something awful like, "Yeah, Monica told me she saw you there."

Blessedly, he didn't. Instead he nodded, then looked up as our server brought two tall, sweating glasses of sweet tea to the table. "Thank you," he said, then calmly ordered for the both of us. Our usual. Pulled pork sandwiches. Cole slaw. Homemade baked chips. Baked cinnamon apples. As the waitress left, he blinked at me and said, "That's still okay, right? To order for you?"

"Of course, Jackson. Gracious, don't you think we've been married long enough—"

"I know. I just don't know the protocol for married couples who no longer live together but who are going out to dinner to discuss Christmas gifts." He took a sip of his tea around a smile. "I can't seem to find the rules anywhere in the handbook."

Was he baiting me? I honestly couldn't tell, and I wasn't sure I knew him well enough anymore to know. Maybe I'd never known him at all. Maybe I'd spent the last twenty years of my life with a man I'd only gone through the motions with.

I swallowed. "What about Travis? Has he mentioned anything to you?"

Jackson laughed. "What *hasn't* he mentioned to me. That boy has figured out the whole my-birthday-Jesus'-birthday thing and has made a list for himself *and* the Lord."

"And I'm sure he wants nothing but the best . . . for the Lord."

Jackson laughed so hard he nearly snorted.

By the end of dinner, we'd developed a list and a plan for divvying up the financial obligation. Jackson insisted he could pay for everything, but just as quickly I reminded him of the unfairness in that. Two hours, two sandwich platters, and two cups of decaf coffee later, we slid out of the booth and walked toward the front of the restaurant, reaching the doors just as Monica Craig walked in, unescorted.

"My goodness," she purred, more at Jackson than at me. "Aren't you two just about the last people I expected to see out and about tonight."

"Monica," Jackson acknowledged her, but before I could say a word, his hand came to the small of my back, and he all but pushed me out the door.

Monica Craig had been an odd sort of thorn in my flesh since high school.

I never could tell where she stood when it came to Jackson and me. Or, more to the point, where she stood when it came to Jackson. In one breath, she'd told Callie what a gentleman Jackson was and how well prepared for his Sunday school lessons he was, which had relieved me. But in another breath, it seemed she managed to always find a way to flirt with him whenever they were together. Between classes. During lunch. After games.

I never could put my finger on it. Was she being genuine with her "sisterly" affection toward him . . . or did something more calculating lurk under the surface of her "we're just friends" hugs and teases. I had nothing solid to go on, really, so I kept my frustration and concerns to myself.

And Callie, of course.

Then came our senior prom . . .

❄

Spring 1997

"How is it," I demanded of Jackson on the way from the dance to Josie Tucker's father's barn where the party was to continue, "that Monica Craig seemed to be *everywhere* we were tonight?"

Jackson looked across the truck's bench seat long enough to show his confusion. "What are you talking about?"

I removed my wrist corsage and placed it between us on the seat. "Don't tell me you didn't notice. I mean, seriously, Jackson. Sometimes I think that girl has a crush on you a mile wide, and you're the only one who can't see it."

Jackson laughed good-naturedly as he rested his arm on the back of the seat. "Come on. She and I are friends, that's all. We go to church together."

I crossed my arms with a huff. "So? I go to church with—with—Dane Boddiford, but you didn't see him every time we turned around, did you? Hovering like some sort of . . . bird of prey?"

Jackson pulled at the spaghetti strap of my dress. "Come on, now . . ."

I swatted his hand. "Excuse me. What are you trying to do?"

His expression—though his eyes never left the road—turned serious. "I'm trying to get you to slide over here and stop all this."

"I can't," I said, shrugging enough to let him know his fingers were not welcomed on my shoulder at that moment.

"Why not?"

I pulled at my seatbelt. "Hello?"

Jackson lifted the center belt. "Hello? Come on, now," he repeated. "Don't ruin tonight. You know how I feel about you."

Only slightly convinced, I unbuckled my seatbelt anyway and slid over, crushing my corsage between us. Lifting it, I moaned. "Now, look . . ."

His arm came around me. Gently. Coaxing. "Buckle up," he said, his voice tender. "And I'll buy you another one."

I did as told, then smiled. "It's okay," I said, my fingers working with the pink ribbons that swirled around white miniature roses. "I was going to press the flowers anyway."

We drove into the open field next to the Tucker's barn, which Mr. and Mrs. Tucker had strewed with white twinkle lights inside and out. Jackson parked his truck next to Callie's date's car. "I see Ryan and Callie have made it already," I mentioned.

Jackson turned off the truck, looked out, and said, "And near-bout everyone else." Then he turned to me, slid one hand along my jawline, and kissed me in such a way I nearly lost my mind. "I love you, Felicia Stewart," he said, his lips a mere breath from mine. "Don't you ever forget that. And don't you ever be jealous of Monica Craig again." He waited a moment. When I remained silent, he added, "Hear me?"

I nodded.

It was all I could do.

Chapter Eighteen

"I don't know what's got your dander up," Jackson said on the way home from the barbecue restaurant.

"I'm sure you don't," I said, arms and legs crossed, jaw clenched so tight I was sure to need a TMJ specialist by Monday.

"Honestly, Felicia, you are a wonder, you know that?"

My head whipped around to face him. "What does *that* mean?"

"It means," he said without looking at me, "that here we are, parents of three great kids, twenty-one years from all that high school drama, and you still let Monica get you riled up."

I shifted to fully face him. "Are you going to sit there and tell me that her showing up was coincidental? That she just *happened* to come to This Little Piggy on her own?"

"Maybe she was meeting someone there."

"Yeah. You. She looked as smug as—"

"Would you listen to yourself? Seriously?"

"You probably let it slip that we were having dinner there." I turned forward in time to see our home—*my* home—come into view. "Or maybe you told her. Maybe you said, 'Honey, I'm having dinner with Felicia on Friday so we can talk about the kids' Christmas.'"

Jackson pulled the truck in front of the house, and I immediately reached for the door handle. "You have lost your mind, Felicia Morgan."

I popped the door open and unbuckled my seatbelt in one movement before descending from the truck. "That's right. I have. But I lost it a long time ago, Jackson." I started to slam the door shut, but caught myself. "Oh. And you be sure to tell her that my last name is *still* Morgan."

"Meaning?"

"Meaning you best remind her that we are *still* married."

Fury crossed Jackson's face. "I tell you what, woman. When you calm down—when you get your brain back—give me a call. Maybe then we can talk about this like adults."

I slammed the door hard enough that the truck rocked slightly, then stormed up the front porch steps and into the house, grateful, at least, that the first floor greeted me in quiet darkness. If the boys were still up, they were upstairs, at least. I closed the front door slowly, then locked it, aware of Jackson's truck lights cutting through the sidelight windows as he turned in the semicircular driveway, heading out. Back to his mother's where he'd been staying since we'd separated.

Or maybe back to the restaurant. Back to Monica, who waited there for him.

Tears stung my eyes, but I blinked them away. He wasn't going to get the better of me. Not when it came to her. At least, not anymore.

"Mom?"

The voice of my daughter coming from the dark living room startled me. I stepped into the arched doorway. She sat sideways in a wingback chair, bathed in muted light from the outside street lamp. Her pajamaed legs were draped over one of the chair's arms. Her feet, clad in thick fuzzy socks, crossed at the ankles. "Sara?" I reached for the light switch.

"No, don't," she said with a sniffle. "I don't want the light on."

I moved closer to her, dropping my purse in the matching wingback chair before sitting in it. Even in the absence of light I could see that she'd been crying. "What's wrong?" I asked.

She brought an oversized coffee mug I'd not noticed before up to her lips and took a small sip. The aroma of warm milk and cinnamon wafted over and I frowned.

Her comfort drink.

"Billy. He—I—"

The old fear washed over me. My breathing stopped. Had he . . . had *they* . . . and had he then dumped her? "What," I whispered. "What did you do?"

Her eyes widened. "Not *that*." Then she sniffled again as new tears came down her cheeks. "Gosh, Mom. Is that *all* you ever worry about?"

Yes. "No, of course not." I waited until she was ready, which seemed hours but was only a minute.

"He broke up with me, Mom. Billy. Billy broke up with me."

"What? Why?" And why right at right at Christmas? How could he hurt my baby like this? "I thought you two were—I didn't know there was a problem."

"There wasn't." She sniffled. "At least I thought there wasn't. But . . . he wants to—he says he's got so much more school to go before he can get his medical degree and he doesn't see how—how we can keep dating if we're going to have to wait so long to get married."

I didn't know whether to cry with her or sigh in my own relief. "Oh, I see."

"Oh, Mom . . . *I love him so much*," she wailed, broken down from the weight of such heartache. I rose from my chair, stepped over to hers, and gathered her in my arms. Within seconds she sat cradled in my lap, clutching her mug of hot milk, crying as though she'd just lost her best friend.

In some way, I suppose she had.

In some way, I suppose, I had too.

So I cried with her.

I put Sara in my bed, telling her she didn't need to be alone. Once she got settled in, I went into her bedroom and plucked her favorite stuffed animal—Mr. Snuggles—from where the nearly dilapidated bunny lay in a mound of throw pillows on her bed. "Here you go," I said, placing him in her arms.

"Oh, Mom," she whimpered. "You always know the right things to do."

I kissed her temple, then whispered back, "I'm going to take a long, hot soak. I'll be just through that door if you need me."

Sara nodded. "I'm just going to sleep now," she mumbled.

I stood a moment to look at her. I paused, remembering how she'd looked in her crib, thumb stuck between two moist lips. In her toddler bed, soft blond curls crowning her head. As a barely-in-my-teens-but-a-teen-nonetheless—hair long, stringy at times. Freckles fading. And now . . . lashes moist with tears from heartache. Lips in a tiny pout.

She looked so much like her father . . .

After a wistful smile, I went into the bathroom and prepared my bath, complete with lavender salts, in a claw-foot tub. While the tub filled, I lit a candle and turned on the vintage-looking small radio

I kept on my vanity. As orchestrated Christmas music filled the room, I twisted the taps off and stepped in, then sank all the way to my neck, breathing in the scent.

My eyes closed as I gripped the sides of the tub. What a night . . .

❄

2014

Jackson rested against the kitchen counter, holding a cup of coffee with a curl of steam rising upward while I finished the dinner dishes. "I don't think I like the idea of my daughter going out with some boy to a dance."

I gave him my best get-over-yourself look. "Jackson Morgan," I said with a chuckle. "She's fifteen. And it's not *some dance*. It's her first Christmas black-and-white ball."

Jackson shook his head as he brought the cup near his lips. "She's fifteen. What's so great about some guy asking you to a dance at fifteen?"

"Don't you remember fifteen?"

He swallowed hard. "Yes," he said looking at me directly. "Which is why I don't want her going out with—how old is this boy?"

"Sixteen."

Jackson groaned. "It's worse than I thought."

"Jackson . . ."

"I guess it's started, huh?"

I wrung out the dishcloth and laid it over the sink divider. "I guess it has. Besides, she's so excited. We went out after school and bought the dress—which you'll approve of, I promise—and she wants to get her nails done and curl her hair . . ."

He groaned again. "Do we even know this boy? His parents?"

"She's in Holy Hands with him," I said, pouring myself a cup of decaf at the coffee station. "He's a good kid. Besides, I've met his parents and they're very nice people." I sat at the kitchen table and Jackson ambled over to join me. "What's more, Tiffany approves."

"Well, by all means, then." He swallowed another sip of his drink. "Which kid is he?"

"The really tall one. Very blond. Grayson Pearce."

Jackson ran a hand over his head. "Blond is good."

"Fathers . . ."

"I guess there's no way to stop this, is there? She's growing up on us."

I nodded. "Well, there is *one* thing we can do."

Jackson raised his eyes in question.

"I volunteered the two of us as chaperones."

Jackson grinned. "Does Sara know that?"

I grinned back. "She will . . ." I brought the mug to my lips. "Soon enough."

But Sara, always full of surprises, shocked us by being pleased when she learned that Jackson and I were chaperoning her first dance.

"I can't believe I'm so nervous." She held her hands out to demonstrate as I stood behind her and zipped up the flowing knee-length black dress with rhinestone-accented one-inch straps we'd purchased. She stood in front of the floor length mirror in the corner of my bedroom as I smiled at her reflection.

"Well, you look lovely," I said, bringing my hand to fluff the blond hair that hung in spiral curls to her waist. "So what's there to be nervous about?"

She turned to face me. "Mom," she whispered. "What if Grayson tries to kiss me?"

I had to swallow back a giggle. "You don't have to, you know."

Her natural blush overshadowed the light pink she'd brushed on earlier.

"Oh," I said. "I see."

"Now, Mom . . ." Sara grabbed my hands. "Please, *please* don't let Daddy do anything to embarrass me."

We turned and started for the door. "I'll do my best. But you know your father."

"Okay," she said as we neared the landing. "Grayson will be here in ten minutes. Go find Dad now and tell him to *not* say anything to embarrass me when he gets here."

"Sara," I admonished as we descended the staircase. "Would your father do anything to . . . yeah. Okay. I'll find him."

True to his word not to embarrass his daughter that evening, Jackson doted without smothering. He gave firm instructions to Grayson without being overbearing. Once at the dance, he stood at the gymnasium's door as a "bouncer" and gave Sara her space, while

I stood at the refreshment table and doled out fruit punch. Later, as the holiday dance neared its end, Jackson came up behind me and whispered, "This reminds me of prom."

I leaned against the familiarity of him, resting the back of my head on his shoulder. "Remember the party afterward? At the Tuckers' barn?" I pointed to the twinkle lights around the makeshift dance floor. "Remember the lights?"

Jackson spoke lightly into my ear, sending shivers up and down my arms. "I only remember how beautiful you looked."

I turned slightly. "And I remember how you kissed me before we went into the barn." Jackson's eyes widened playfully. "You'd never kissed me like *that* before."

His arms circled my waist and I nestled in. "It was time. If I remember correctly, we'd been arguing about some girl—"

I turned again, mouth opened. "Some girl, my eye. You know good and well—"

Jackson placed a finger to my lips. "Now, now Mrs. Morgan. Don't make me kiss you like *that* again in front of all these children . . ."

Chapter Nineteen

Christmas Season 2018

I tiptoed past my sleeping daughter, her arms still wrapped around Mr. Snuggles, her cheeks flushed from crying, and into the hallway, then down the stairs where my purse still lay in the wingback chair. After pulling out my phone, I called Jackson, then held my breath, wondering if he would bother to answer.

"I'm too tired for round two," he said as a sleepy hello.

"I'm not calling for that," I said, keeping my voice low. "I wanted you to know that Sara came home early. She—she um . . . she's pretty upset. Billy broke up with her today."

Jackson sighed deeply from the other end. "Oh, man. Did she say why?"

"Something about it being too long between marriage and his degree or some such nonsense. But she—"

When I didn't finish my thought, he asked, "What? She what?"

"Well," I said, easing back in the chair, "She indicated that—I don't think anything has, you know, *happened* between them."

His groan lasted what felt like a full minute. "Felicia, honestly. Is that all you ever worry about?"

I frowned. Out of the three of us—them and me—which of us was right? *Could* it be as they'd always said? Had I let my fears get the better of me? Had it tainted my views on everything? "Now you sound like Sara," I admitted. Or had she sounded like him?

"At least she's still got her good sense then. And if I know our daughter, like her old man, she'll pull herself up by her bootstraps and be fine. By this time tomorrow, Billy what's-his-name will be just that. Nothing but a faint memory."

Like her old man?

"Is that what's happened with us? Have you pulled yourself up by your bootstraps? Are you fine without us?"

He growled. "Felicia—"

"Jackson, I didn't call to have a tug of war with words." I crossed my legs.

"Then why *did* you call?"

"Because," I said as though my reasoning should be obvious. "Sara is your daughter too. And I thought you'd want to know."

"Of course I want to know."

"And for your information, *that* is not all I worry about. I just don't want—"

"What?" he asked. And when I didn't answer—when I *couldn't* answer for the knot forming in my throat—he answered for me. "You don't want her to end up like you? Pregnant and married? Not because she's in love and can't see the raw future for the stars in her eyes but because it's expected of her? My gosh, Felicia, I thought we'd gotten past all that. I thought we'd built something and built it out of nothing. Those kids of ours didn't come out of three one-night stands, you know."

My jaw flexed. "I don't have to sit here and listen to this, Jackson. I only wanted you to know—"

"Thank you, then. Thank you for telling me. I'll come by in the morning before work to check on her."

"I doubt she'll be awake . . ."

"Then I'll text her in the morning and see if she wants to meet for lunch." He waited a breath before adding. "Leesha . . ."

"What," I whispered.

"Don't think for one minute that I haven't been in love with you since senior year. That night—the night after Dad died—may not have been our wisest move, but I don't regret it. Not for one second." I squeezed my eyes shut against his words. Hot tears pushed past my lashes and made their way down my cheeks. "I can only pray that one day you'll feel the same way. One thing I've learned in all this is that God uses everything, Felicia. Even our mess-ups."

With that, he hung up, leaving me nearly breathless. Gasping in tiny air pockets that didn't quite reach my lungs. For the second time that night, I cried, this time until my head throbbed from the pressure. And, when I'd nearly dehydrated myself, I stood, walked over to the special ornament bin, and rummaged around until I found the little black dress ornament Jackson had given me the year of Sara's first dance. "There has never been nor will there ever be a more beautiful woman in a little black dress," he'd said as I pulled the shimmering ornament of cut champagne-glass sequins from my stocking. When I held it up and watched the lights reflect from it, he added, "than you."

I clutched it now, feeling the rough edges dig into the flesh of my hand as the final words of our phone conversation rushed over me.

Don't think for one minute that I haven't been in love with you since senior year. I can only pray that one day you'll feel the same way.

"He said that?" Callie asked me early the next afternoon from the comfort of the understated sunroom in the back of her home. We had both curled at opposite ends of a loveseat, our hands wrapped around a cup of hot cocoa. "He said he's been in love with you since senior year?"

I blew tiny marshmallows across a chocolate sea as I nodded. "And that he prayed one day I'd feel the same way."

Callie's stare burned nearly as hot as my first sip of the drink she'd offered ten minutes before. "What?" I asked, catching her eyes and raised brow.

"Do you?"

I lowered the mug to my lap. "For heaven's sake, Callie. He's my husband. The father of my children."

Her face softened. "I didn't ask if he was your husband, Leesha. I asked if you're in love with him."

The grip I had on the cup's handle tightened. "Callie . . . how can you ask me something like that?"

"Then let me rephrase the question—have you *ever* been in love with Jackson?"

"Of course. We couldn't have made it this far if—"

"Then why are you always so angry with him?"

I stood quickly—almost too quickly—then balanced the cocoa as I headed for the kitchen, Callie right behind me. "Now you're angry with me," she said.

I placed my half-consumed drink on the granite countertop and turned to face her. "I'm not angry."

She placed both hands on mine and drew me closer, pulling my arms taut. "You are my best friend and I love you to pieces, but I'm going to tell you the truth here whether you like it or not . . ."

"By all means," I said, looking down, noting her elegant pear-shaped engagement ring and its matching wedding band against the simplicity of mine. A thin gold band, which had been the best we could afford at nineteen and broke. But when we could afford more—and when Jackson mentioned buying me a diamond—I'd balked. Why pretend something that never happened or ever would? I'd never get the down-on-one-knee moment. I wouldn't hear, "Will you marry me?" My memories would only consist of a fear-stricken face that suddenly became composed as the man behind it said, "I guess we'll have to get married, then. Is that what you're thinking?"

It was and it wasn't. I didn't truthfully know what I was thinking other than that my father was going to kill one or both of us and that Mrs. Morgan had been through enough without the scandal of an unmarried son, his pregnant girlfriend, and a grandchild born out of wedlock.

So Jackson and I purchased simple gold bands to go with our simple ceremony and our simple studio apartment.

And never once had I removed it. Not to wash dishes. Not when it grew tight with pregnancy. And not after he packed an oversized bag one morning while the kids were asleep and said, "I can't do this anymore, Felicia. I can't keep this up," while I stood in the center of our bedroom, too numb to protest. Too tired to fight and uncertain of anything beyond that moment except that when Monica Craig moved back from LA, my world turned on its head.

Callie tugged on my arms again. "But, you *are* angry with Jackson," she said, reminding me of the topic at hand.

"It's that Monica Craig," I said, my head jerking up.

"It's *not* Monica Craig." She squeezed my hands. "Come on. You *have* to figure this out, Leesh."

I slid my hands from hers. "If you are so all-fired smart, Callie, why don't you just *tell* me what it is."

She shook her head. "I can't. You have to figure this out on your own."

Honestly. Between her and Treva and Jackson, all three of them with their riddles, one would think we were in elementary school. "That makes little to no sense."

"It makes perfect sense. No matter what I tell you right now, you'll argue with me about it or you'll deny it. One or both. *You* have to figure this out." She gathered me in her arms and held me tightly enough that I couldn't free myself. "I just hope you figure it out before it's too late."

CHAPTER TWENTY

When I returned home, Sara stood in the middle of the foyer, arms crossed and the toe of her ankle boots tapping.

"What?" I said, closing the door behind me. "Did something happen when you had lunch with your dad? What did he say?" I looked toward the stairs. "Where's Hank?"

She crooked her finger, indicating I should follow her as she walked into the living room. "Look at this tree," she said, then threw her arms up in defeat. "And he's across the street playing with Mikey."

I shrugged out of my coat. "Oh," I said, then looked at the tree. "What about it?"

"Mom, you've had all week to put up nineteen ornaments. I could have done the whole thing in ten minutes but you've only put up . . ." She pretended to count the few ornaments on the tree.

I frowned. "I'll get it done." I started for the coat tree in the foyer. "When?"

I turned to look at her, my hands gripping the coat. "By tomorrow. Monday at the latest. I promise. Besides, I didn't think you'd be back until later today so . . ."

"Mom." She took steps toward me, the heels of her boots clomping on the hardwood floor. "I told you I'd do this if you needed me to. I know every one of those ornaments means something to you, and I know where they go. I promise to give them their proper place."

"No, no." I hung my coat, then faced her and pretended to smile. "I really want to do it . . . it's just a little more cathartic than I expected. Speaking of which . . . how are you feeling today?"

Sara nodded as she rocked back and forth as though she were preparing for a dance step. "Dad thinks Billy will come around. He gave me the whole love-something-let-it-go speech."

If you love something, let it go . . .

I have been in love with you since high school . . .

"And what do you think?" I asked, pushing the words from my thoughts as I started for the kitchen with Sara trailing behind me.

"I think I'm going to do exactly what Dad suggested."

"Which is?" I opened the refrigerator and removed a packet of chicken thighs.

She blinked several times before placing her hands on her narrow hips and giving the world a nod. "I'm going to concentrate on having a happy holiday with myself, my immediate family, and my friends," she said, as though she'd rehearsed the words from lunch to that very moment. "And I'm going to start tonight. I called Tiff. She and I are going to catch a movie and then go out for a burger."

I held the chicken higher. "So no dinner here?"

Sara wrinkled her nose. "No. Is that okay?"

Again, I forced a smile. "Sure."

"And you can get on with those remaining ornaments." She started for the door. "I need to get ready." She paused near the old farmhouse table. "Oh, did I tell you that Tiff and Grayson Pearce are a thing now?"

My eyes widened. "You're kidding."

"Nope," she chuckled. "Remember when I thought Grayson hung the moon?"

"And you were so hopeful for that first kiss?"

She laughed. "Oh, yeah . . . his was the first." She shrugged. "See? Sooner or later, they all leave me. First Grayson, now Billy."

I chuckled with her, then shook my head. Jackson had been right the night before. She'd always been so much like him . . . able to take whatever life gave—no matter how many lemons and no matter how sour—and turn them into the proverbial lemonade stand.

❉

February 2017

"I've decided," Jackson said between bites of another late-night supper.

"What's that?" I sat across the table from him as I'd so often done over the years, watching him eat alone while the children got ready for bed or did their homework, and I waited to clean up one more round of dishes.

"The store is doing really well, Leesh . . ."

That didn't surprise me, especially with all the long hours he put in, the expanding of product lines he'd thought to add, and the way he'd spruced up the interior of the store. Somehow, he'd managed to combine an auto parts store with a sporting goods center and come up with a unique package.

I tilted my head. "And you've made so much money you want to take me on a cruise around the world," I half-teased.

His eyes widened. "What? No . . ."

"I was teasing." Sort of. Between work, the house, the kids, and one typically absent husband, I'd hit a wall of drudgery and exhaustion.

Jackson swallowed down a half glass of sweet tea in three gulps. "No . . . I'm thinking of expanding."

I tried to wrap my brain around the words as I went to grab the tea pitcher from the fridge. "What does that mean? You've got auto parts, you've got sporting goods . . . what else is there? Swimwear? Diamonds from Tiffany's?" I refilled his glass, then placed the pitcher on the table between us.

His arms rested against the edge of the table as I returned to my seat. "Are you going to listen or are you going to keep saying silly stuff like that?"

I couldn't tell if he was being cute or had grown impatient. "Sorry."

"No, seriously," he continued as though he'd erased the last minute and a half of conversation. "You know I've always wanted to take Morgan's to some of the other towns around here. Maybe even put one in Savannah."

"Savannah?"

"Actually, my accountant thinks that's where I ought to start, but I don't know . . ." He wiped his mouth with the napkin he'd kept wadded in his left hand. "What do you think?"

"Jackson, Sara will start college soon and Trav won't be far behind her. Can we afford this?"

He shook his head. Pushed his plate away. "Leesh, you're always worried about money. Remember when we bought our first house?"

"What about it?"

"You were so worried about whether or not we could afford it. Same with everything we've done. Getaways. Furniture. Even with the babies. *Can we afford another child?*"

I stood, reaching for his plate. "Well, someone around here has to be levelheaded."

Jackson grabbed my wrist and pulled me into his lap, then locked his arms around my hips. I pushed against him, but he only held on tighter. "Been a while since I held you like this," he said, smiling. "Miss Levelhead."

I looked him in the eye as I raised my brow. "It's hard to hold your wife when you're never home," I reminded him. "Level head or not."

He kissed the hollow of my throat, and my legs went to tingles despite my resolve not to be effected by his cuteness. "I'll do better," he whispered. "I promise."

I skootched a notch toward his knees to face him better. "Jackson, how are you going to *do better* if you open new locations? You'll be gone more than ever."

He inched me closer. "I'll delegate." He shifted me so I was forced to put my head on his shoulder. "I've already talked to my associate manager about taking over the Bakersville store while I look into starting another one. And I really do think starting in Savannah is the best bet."

"I can see it now," I mumbled. "You'll call at night, telling me you can't make it back home and letting me know you'll just get some hotel room for the night." I closed my eyes. "Next thing I know, you've got a whole other family over there and you're living a double life."

Jackson leaned his head back and laughed. "Gracious, I can barely keep my arms around this wife without her trying to wiggle away. What would I want with another?"

I couldn't bear it. Couldn't stand his adorableness another second. I wrapped my arms around his shoulders and laid a kiss on his neck. "Jackson," I whispered. "If you do this, *please* make me a part of it. Talk to me about what you're doing and how you're doing it."

"Keep kissing me like that," he said, "and I promise, I will."

But his promise was only as good as that night. Soon enough, Jackson did exactly what I'd feared. Between realtors and contractors and driving back and forth to Savannah, along with the occasional "I'll get a hotel room . . . kiss the kids for me" nights, I began to feel like a single mother.

The Savannah location opened six months after he made his breakable promise. The children and I, along with Callie and Taylor and my dad, were there for the ribbon cutting, the balloons, and the hot dog vendor.

Jackson offered a grand opening sale with plenty of giveaways. People came by in droves and, while I couldn't have been prouder, by the end of the day, I stood on the opposite side of the store sipping on a coke from the 1950s-style soda fountain Jackson had envisioned as a "cool idea."

Callie stood next to me, sucking soda through a red and white striped straw. "Where in the world did he come up with this notion?" she asked after swallowing, indicating with her eyes the counter with its swivel stools and the pimple-faced soda jerk.

"Muscle cars of the fifties," I said. "Didn't you know that souped-up Chevys and Corvettes and Packards go with poodle skirts and soda shops?"

"Well, I suppose I didn't. But it's an ingenious idea." She took another swallow. "I haven't had a soda or a float from a real fountain in—" Her brows knit together. "How long?" She shrugged. "I think that time our class took that field trip to the World of Coca-Cola in Atlanta right after it opened. Remember?"

I didn't answer; my eyes were on my oldest children—Sara, now eighteen by only a few weeks, and Travis, twelve—and the easy way they moved behind the counter and interacted with the customers. "They are evermore his children," I said before hiking myself up and onto a stool. It swiveled on its own according until I caught the chrome foot rail with the toe of my sandal.

Callie followed my lead. "Did Jackson ever hire someone to manage this store?"

I looked around until I saw a tall, dark-skinned man who Jackson had introduced earlier in the day. "That's Morris over there," I said with a discreet point. "As soon as Jackson feels he's ready, he's promised me he'll let him take over."

"Ah," she said about the same time my father and Taylor ambled over.

"Well," Dad said. "He did it."

"Yes, he did," I said, forcing yet another smile. "Just like he said he would." More or less. "And in six months' time."

"The kids are in their element," Taylor commented. "Even little Hank has his father's stance down pat."

I stretched my back to look around. "Where *is* he?"

"Don't worry," Dad answered. "He hasn't left Jackson's side since he and I got here two hours ago." Dad looked at Taylor. "Mr. Reddick, can I buy you a drink?" he said with a wink.

"Well, I believe you can, Dr. Stewart," Taylor answered, grinning.

Callie and I exchanged a look and a sigh before my eyes went in search of my absent husband one more time.

Chapter Twenty-One

"Are you coming home tonight?" I asked Jackson in the quiet of the manager's office, when the last customer had left the new store and the only employee who remained was Morris.

Jackson shook his head and pretended to be sad, even when I could see the excitement of the past few hours shining in the crystal of his eyes. "Sweetie, I gotta be here so early in the morning, I thought I'd just—"

"—get a hotel room," I finished for him. I crossed my arms. Looked at my feet. "Yeah."

He brought his arms around me and I stiffened. "Okay, Leesh. I deserve it. I know."

"It's Saturday," I reminded him. "Tomorrow is Sunday. You don't open the stores on Sunday."

"I know . . . but Morris and I—"

"And what about church?"

He shrugged. "So, I'll miss a Sunday. Sweetheart . . ."

"You promised," I said. "And you said you'd make me a part of it all."

"I know."

"But I don't recall you asking me about anything. I'm not stupid, Jackson. I could have helped."

He kissed the top of my head. "What would you have done?"

I shrugged. "I don't know. I could have helped with . . . the fifties design. Believe it or not, I know a little bit about that era. I watched *Grease*."

He chuckled, but I didn't laugh with him. Instead I wiggled free of his embrace. "I gotta get Hank home," I said, looking at our son who slept, mouth open, on the leather loveseat beneath the observation window.

"Here," he said. "Let me carry him to the car."

I glanced at my phone on the way to the parking lot as the low country summer air slapped me in the face like a wet washcloth. Sara and Travis had left thirty minutes earlier. I'd told her not to stop anywhere on the way home, and the tracking app indicated she'd done exactly that. Hopefully she'd be at the house long before I arrived.

"They'll be there," Jackson said, reading my mind.

I hated when he did that and told him so.

He only chuckled as he shook Hank lightly. "Hey, buddy," he said. "You gotta help me get you into your booster."

I opened the back passenger's door as Hank's eyes opened halfway, then closed against any will of his own. "Huh?" he said.

Jackson worked to get him in as I walked around to the driver's side. "Don't get in yet," Jackson said, his voice barely a whisper. "I want to tell you—"

"I want to start the air," I said. "Hank will melt if I don't."

Jackson nodded. I slid behind the steering wheel, started the car, and then closed the door. My skin had turned slick with perspiration and immediately turned to gooseflesh with the first blast of cold air. Seeing Jackson now standing at the window, I lowered it. He bent at the waist and leaned in. "Leesha," he said. "I know I didn't keep you in the loop. But you had other things— more important things—to deal with."

"Like what, Jackson?"

"Like the kids. And all that research you have to do at work. And keeping up the house. What part of that would you have left behind to come running over here to pick out shelving or paint or . . . neon-lighted Route 66 signs?"

"What time will you be home tomorrow?" I asked, leaving his question where it belonged.

"Midafternoon." He held up two fingers like the Boy Scout he had been. "I promise. I owe you that much."

I narrowed my eyes, feeling a new anger rise up, but forcing it back down. "Don't be any later," I said. "I mean it, Jackson."

He kissed me, lightly. "I promise, Leesh." He kissed me again. "And thank you."

"For what?" For going home? For not making a stink right here in a darkened, steaming-hot parking lot?

"For everything," he answered. "I know you don't believe it, but I couldn't have done all this without you." He started to pull out of the car, then stopped. "Hey—"

I raised my brow in question.

"Do you think . . ." His eyes grew misty and he shook his head. "What?"

Even in the muted light from the streetlamp I could see him swallow hard. "Do you think Dad would be proud right now?"

My heart grew heavy before it turned to a puddle. "Jackson," I whispered as I placed a hand on the side of his face. "He would have been proud of you, even without all this."

Something flickered in his eyes. Something beyond what I'd seen in the past within their see-through blue color. Something beyond the laughter that danced within them. "Thank you for that," he finally said. "I love you so much."

This time I kissed him. "I love you too."

And I meant every word of it. As I reached Bakersville's city limits, Hank continued to sleep, my radio played easy listening, and I began to stew in an anger I couldn't put my finger on. Not right away, anyway.

The knotting in my stomach started as I turned out of the parking lot and then folded in with angst. Together, they simmered. Words ping-ponged in my head and my heart in such a way that I found myself unable to keep up with them.

Something he had said . . .

I went over each word, each line spoken from the time I'd arrived at the store until I'd seen the hope in his eyes and told him I loved him. And in spite of the tenderness of the moment, there was something there, something that made me want to slam the palms of my hands against the steering wheel and shriek until I had no air left in my lungs.

Not that I would.

A glance to the back seat reminded me that my son—*our* son— slept peacefully with a tiny line of drool from his pouty lips to his jawline. Another sweet product of a night where everything wrong in the world seemed right, and Jackson and I were one in a way I believed so few could be.

They'll be there . . . he'd said, reading my concerns about our older children as only he could. Knowing I worried. What if they stopped off for a burger? Or Sara got on the phone with Billy while Travis played on his phone and neither of them paid attention?

Jackson had always been so certain of everything, including how well the kids would turn out while I never seemed to stop fretting. Because something . . . *something* . . . always needled at me. Poked me in places that hurt beyond measure and yet in places I couldn't always reach. Or find.

But Jackson . . . Jackson always . . . Jackson . . .

"He thinks he knows me so well," I said aloud, then stole another glance to the back seat. Hank's head had shifted from the right to the left, but his eyes remained closed, his lashes thick against his soft cheeks.

Do you think Dad would be proud?

"*Mom,*" I heard myself saying to my mother shortly before her death. "*I'd like to get a degree in interdisciplinary studies . . . maybe go on to be a lawyer . . . or . . .*"

"*Jackson,*" I had said more than once, "*I'm thinking about going back to school.*"

Jackson was living his dream. Jackson *had been* living his dream while I'd been driving children to school and soccer and Holy Hands and church and ballet and football. Jackson had taken that stupid, sour lemon and made a lemonade stand while I worked at a law office—which I'd always thought close enough to my dream—and cooked and cleaned and got baths and brushed teeth and made sure homework was done and prayers said and . . .

I swung the car into our driveway, bringing it to a stop behind Sara's truck. Yes, yes. The kids had made it home without incident. Jackson knew us all so well. But I now knew he hadn't known me quite as well as he thought.

Until that moment, neither had I.

CHAPTER TWENTY-TWO

The next day, we went to Dad's after church for Sunday dinner.

"Where's Jackson?" he asked when I found him in the kitchen. Hank ran around me and threw himself into his grandfather's arms.

"Savannah," I answered.

"You're kidding," he said from around the squeeze he gave to his youngest grandson, then scooted him back to the family room so he could "talk to your mama."

Sounds of a televised baseball pregame started up from behind me. "Trav," I called over my shoulder. "Turn that down a decibel."

"Sorry," he called back.

I looked back at Dad. "No, I'm not," I said before reaching into the cabinet for a glass.

"And if I know my daughter—and I do—you are none too happy about that fact." Dad reached into the refrigerator and brought out the iced tea pitcher and a plate of burgers.

I took the pitcher and prepared a glass of tea. "Want one?" I asked.

"Already got one," he said, nodding toward a glass I hadn't noticed.

"Dad?" I began, then took a sip and placed the glass on the counter. "Do you think it's too late for me to go back to school?"

Dad paused, studying me. "I don't think it's ever too late. But what are *your* thoughts?"

I crooked my finger, letting Dad know that I wanted him to follow me. We walked from the kitchen, through the dining room and living room, and then down a long hallway, past bedrooms and baths, and into one richly paneled room Dad referred to as his "library."

"Felicia," he said behind me. "What are we doing? I've got burgers to cook."

"Look," I said, pointing to the wall behind the massive desk, which sat in the middle of the room and faced the door. "What do you see?"

"My diplomas," he answered matter-of-factly.

I walked around the desk, sat in the tufted soft-leather chair, my hands resting over the arms. "Do you know," I began, then swiveled the chair to face the wall, "that when I was a little girl, I used to come in here. Sit. Look up at these diplomas." I swung around again. My father had slid his hands into his khaki pants pockets. His face looked unsure, as if I'd just relayed news he'd never expected to hear. "I used to sit and think about what mine would look like, maybe even hanging next to yours." I stood and walked toward him. "Having a diploma was *everything* because I wanted you—I wanted you and Mom to be proud—" Just as Jackson hoped his father would have been proud, had he lived to see the accomplishments of his youngest son.

"Sweetheart—"

"No, Dad. Just listen. I *know* you're proud of me no matter what—"

"You've done amazing things, Leesh. You and Jackson both."

I shook my head. He didn't get it. He couldn't fully understand. He'd gone to college. Met Mom. Graduated and *then* got married. They'd waited two years before getting pregnant with me. He'd done it all . . . *his* way. "I wanted to go to college." I raised my hands. "And I know that I went. But, if you remember, I wanted to go Georgia—"

"Yes, but I think your wanting to go there may have had more to do with Jackson than academics."

"Granted, but it was still a dream. A dream I never got to finish." I sat up straighter. "And before you say anything, I know I went to Southern, but what I wanted more than going was—I wanted to *finish* college. I wanted to have a career in law, but what I got was a *job* and . . . who knows? If I could have stayed the course, in time, maybe I would have even gone back to get my JD." I looked down at my father's desk, to the chaos of papers and pens and paper clips and books on veterinary medicine. "I love my kids," I whispered, tears now stinging my eyes.

Dad crossed the room to wrap me in his arms while I squeezed my eyes to keep the tears from continuing. "I know you do. And you're a good mother. A great mother."

"And I wouldn't trade them . . ."

"I know you wouldn't."

"But, Dad—"

He stepped back. "Felicia, isn't what you do enough? Isn't it exactly what you would have done with the degree you went to Southern to get in the first place? What you're doing now?"

"It's just a piece of paper. I know. But it says I accomplished something. And I know that the firm has personally trained me and sent me to a few workshops and—that's just it, Dad. When I was at those workshops . . . when I sat in those classrooms and listened to the instructors . . . I remembered being back at Southern and I *so* wanted to—" I shook my head. "No one ever asked me, really."

"Asked you what?"

I pointed to my chest. "What *I* wanted to do. It was just assumed. And I—I was too shocked by my own behavior and my own circumstances to think it through." I took a breath. "Jackson and I made the right decision, Dad. I do believe that. I'm just wondering now if it was the only decision."

❄

December 1998

As soon as I pulled into the restaurant's parking lot—the little diner Jackson suggested we meet—I spotted him through the large window. Sitting in a booth. Head down. Shoulders slumped.

He knew. He had figured out why I wanted to talk to him. Why I would drive three-and-a-half hours to see him, six weeks after the fact.

Jackson turned then, looked out the window, and saw me too. He gave a funny sort of half smile, held up one hand in a mock wave, and I took a deep breath. The time had come. I had rehearsed all the way from Statesboro, saying, "I'm pregnant," in about every conceivable way. But now, only time would tell how I'd actually say those two, hypocritical words.

How is it, I wondered as I stepped out of the car, that the same simple line—I'm pregnant—could spark such joy or such fear, such excitement or such anguish? How could they be both the words that ignited hope for a future or fear of being trapped by it?

I opened the café door and walked on shaky legs to where Jackson now slid out of the booth. "Hey," he drew out, then leaned down to kiss my cheek as though we were old friends who happened to meet up in a student-driven restaurant that played music a hair too loud from overhead speakers.

The waitress sauntered over as soon as we sat. Jackson already had an oversized glass of half-consumed coke in front of him, so I said I'd have the same. Mainly because I needed to keep this meeting simple. Uncomplicated.

"Are you eating?" the waitress asked, more to Jackson than me. I waited for his cue. "Leesh?" he asked.

I exhaled nervous laughter. Jackson had always ordered for us both. Had always known what I wanted. How had so much changed? "Uh—no. Just a coke."

Jackson lifted his chin to the waitress. "We're good," he said.

As she walked away, I studied his face. And, I suppose, he studied mine. Both of us giving the other the floor but neither of us speaking. The waitress returned with my drink. I thanked her and she walked away.

"I guess you heard I'm dropping out of college."

Prickles of confusion rushed over me. "What? *No . . .*"

"It's the right thing to do."

The right thing.

I wrapped my hands around the sweating drink while Jackson picked up the straw the waitress had left beside it. He tore the top precisely, then shoved the paper down as he'd done countless times in our dating life. He slipped the straw into my drink. "Here you go," he said, which was what he'd always said.

Jackson. Steady as a rock. Sure as the sun. Always.

"But why?" I asked.

He grimaced against an inner torment. "Mom—Mom said she was going to sell Morgan's. I couldn't—I can't let that happen, Leesh." Tears formed in his eyes. "That store meant everything to Dad. If she were to sell it to someone who didn't put the same love and care into it that he—well." He shrugged. "We've set something up where I can purchase it by making payments to Mom, which will give her some spending money. You know, that kind of thing." Jackson paused long enough to give a nod of confidence. "I can do this, Leesh. I can run Morgan's and I can make an even better success of it than Dad did." He exhaled, and with the air came the tiniest touch of self-assuredness. "I know I can."

"But what about your education? Your degree?"

"It's just a piece of paper. I'm here studying business." His brow crinkled. "Well, some things you can't teach. Some things you just have to do to learn."

I took a long sip of my drink, felt it tickle and burn. But I didn't say anything. I didn't know what to say. He'd just lost his beloved father. Now he felt the pressure of losing something that meant the world to the man who meant the world to him. And here I was, about to drop another burden onto his broad shoulders that looked as though they'd fold in two.

Jackson stared out the window for a minute, his jawline flexing, his lips drawn thin. "Besides . . . between the three of us kids, I'm the only one who can do it, you know? I'm the only one still in Bakersville. The only one not committed already to a job or a family."

I nodded as he continued to stare, his eyes unfocused. He raked his teeth over his bottom lip, and then his head whipped back and his eyes found mine. "And I guess you're here to tell me you're pregnant, right?"

CHAPTER TWENTY-THREE

It made no sense to say something lame like, "How did you guess?"

Of course he'd guessed. He was an adult, nearly. He could count.

Still, I took another sip of my drink as I nodded, keeping my gaze to the table. To the shiny black specs in the red linoleum. When I looked up, I found him staring at me, his skin chalky, his eyes a washed-out blue. I nodded again in case he'd missed the first one.

The color returned and he nodded back. "I guess we'll get married then. Is that what you're thinking?"

"I haven't—I honestly haven't thought that far. I mean, I suppose I could just . . . you don't have to . . . there are even day care centers near Southern and I—"

"Makes sense."

"What? The day care center?"

His eyes grew wide. "No. Getting married," he said it as if that were that. No more discussion. No laying out the options. Not that, deep down, I expected anything else from Jackson. At the core of him, that was who he was. This was the son who planned to drop out of college to make sure his father's store wasn't sold to someone who wouldn't care enough to keep it afloat. To make it successful. Yes, Jackson had made a mistake, a lack in judgment, but as in everything expected of him, he would own up to it.

"Oh," I said.

His brow furrowed. "So . . . you're what? About six weeks?"

"Mmmhmm. The doctor I went to—there's this free clinic on campus, not that it matters—well, she said I'm due late July. Early August."

Jackson's eyes darted back and forth. "Yeah. That would be about right." Then he blinked. "Are you okay? I mean, sick or anything?"

"What do you mean *that would be about right*?"

Now his face turned crimson. "You know . . . since . . ."

"What did you think, Jackson? That if I were further along it wouldn't be—"

"No," he said a little too loudly. He swallowed hard. "No," he repeated, this time with control.

I bent forward, drawing my hands under the table, and then clasping them together. "Because you know that one time was the *first* time . . . the only . . ."

He sat back. "I know," he mouthed, and his face turned a different shade of red. Then he leaned in. "This was my fault. I want to make this right, Leesh." His brows went up, forming a peak where they met. "Please, just let me make this right."

"I guess it makes sense." I reached up and pushed my drink away, unable to tolerate another swallow. "There's no reason I can't finish out this semester and, once the baby's born—"

"Have you told your dad yet?"

"You're still alive, aren't you?"

Jackson actually chuckled. "I'll take that as a no." He looked out the window again, then back at me. "I think a lot of him. I'm so, so sorry. He doesn't deserve—*you* don't deserve—"

"And what about your mom? She's been through so much . . . losing your dad."

He shook his head as sorrow masked the handsomeness of his face. That same sorrow I'd seen before. On that night. That one night. "I guess I really did it, didn't I? I guess I really mucked things up." He sighed. "Not just for you and me but for everyone. And here I thought I knew better." His eyes met mine. "Since that night, Leesh, I've prayed every night. Asking God to forgive me—"

"I have too. I mean, me. Asking Him to forgive me."

Another line creased his brow. "Not you. You shouldn't have had to. This was on me. All of it. And I told God that too. I couldn't—I know I should have called you since I got back to Athens, but I—I was just so—"

"The phone works both ways, Jackson. If I'm being honest, I didn't want you to call. I think we needed this time . . . not talking. Not pretending it was something it wasn't." I squeezed my hands together again, not wanting to discuss blame further. Mainly because it was pointless but in part because I'd already done enough of it. I'd had more time to process the ominous news. To go from fear to anger, where blame takes residency, and back to fear again. But not for a single moment had I considered the possibility of what would happen after revealing the news. Even though, surely, *something* would. "So . . . what's the plan, then?" I asked the only person at the table who seemed certain enough of anything at all to know. "When do you want to tell them?"

"Well," he said after a moment of thinking, "what are you doing the rest of the weekend?"

I didn't have a single plan beyond that moment. Beyond driving to Athens and telling Jackson as I'd already done. Plans complete. After that? "Nothing."

Jackson slid out of the booth and extended his hand. I reached out, tentatively at first, but then placed mine in his as though what we were about to do was the most natural thing in the world. As if we were about to bring our parents the happiest of news rather than one bent on rocking their world. "Come on, then," he said. "We may as well get it over with."

❄

August 2017

"No one really asked me," I said to my father as we stood in his study. "No one said, 'How do you feel about leaving school, getting married, having a baby . . . ?' No one."

Dad wagged his finger at me. "That's not true, Felicia. I distinctly remember walking into your bedroom that night—the night you and Jackson drove from Athens to tell Karen and me—"

I exhaled. "Poor Mrs. Morgan. I've never ever seen anyone look so stricken—"

"I went into your room," Dad continued, now pointing toward my bedroom, "and I asked you if this was what you wanted." He lifted my chin to look at him. "And what did you say, young lady?"

My nineteen-year-old self returned with the subtle endearment. I had become a teenager again in my childhood home, my father standing before me, demanding that I be honest with myself, if with no one else. "I said—I said that yes, I was sure."

"I would have supported you in any decision, Leesha." His head bobbed slightly. "Well, in almost every decision. You know how I feel about—"

"I know. I just didn't—Dad, I couldn't *see* myself as one of those girls who walks around campus ginormously pregnant with no ring on her finger." I crossed my arms. "Of course, I didn't see myself as the kind of girl who got pregnant before she got married, either."

"Well," Dad said, his toe kicking at some nonexistent something on the carpet, "you weren't the first, and you most assuredly won't be the last."

That much had proven to be true. Not a year after Jackson and I shocked Bakersville, Lacey Henry and Colton Stembridge did the same. Of course, they'd both had a reputation for living on the edge, so—. "Tell me what to do, Dad."

"Have you told Jackson?"

"That I want to go back to school? Yes. But, years ago."

"Come on," Dad said, turning toward the door. "I gotta get those burgers going."

"Dad . . ."

He stopped. Looked at me. "Tell your husband, Felicia. Tell him you want to finish your degree. There are online courses now, which shouldn't make things too difficult."

"Yeah," I said. "I've wondered about that. All right, then," I said, feeling lighter and readier to face the real giant. "I'll tell him. Today, when he gets home."

Dad shook his head and chuckled as he turned and started down the hallway. "Gracious, Felicia, you make the biggest mountains out of the smallest molehills."

A sentiment held by both of the men in my life. And Dad was right; Jackson had no qualms at all about me going back to school. By the time he returned home, late, I'd gone online and looked up the necessities to complete my degree. Jackson looked at my notes, nodded, and said, "Sure. If that's what you want."

Then he turned. "I'm going to go shower," he said.

I raised a brow toward his exit. But I smiled at the piece of paper he'd tossed back onto the kitchen table as though it bore only the most casual of notes. "You do that," I said. And then I did a private little happy dance no one could see.

Chapter Twenty-Four

Thanksgiving 2017

By Thanksgiving, Morgan's in Savannah was up and running at full steam. Jackson drove over once a week to keep a check on things, worked in the Bakersville store four days a week, and spent a sixth day each week working on the specs for the next location.

We were down one child in the house. Sara had been accepted to Southern, which thrilled her because that had been her first choice, and tickled me absolutely pink because—while she'd be living in the dorm—she could easily come home most weekends.

"She'll be far enough away to feel grown up," Jackson noted one night soon after we got her settled in and then drove back home. We lay in bed, shoulders touching, and the backs of our heads planted into the middle of our pillows. "But not so far away that we can't get to her if we have to."

"Faux independence," I said. "Not that she'll know it until she has one of her own go off to college."

Jackson turned his head toward mine. "One down . . ."

I smiled, too tired to laugh. "Don't even think it. Don't even talk to me about the boys leaving one day. I can hardly bear *this*."

"Well," he said closing his eyes, "we've got a while to go before the nest is completely empty. And by then . . . who knows? Sara will be married already and bringing her little rug rats over to terrorize us."

I jabbed at his rib cage and he smiled, though he kept his eyes closed. "Not tonight, sweetheart," he teased. "I'm too tired."

"Very funny."

I flipped over on my side, my back to my husband. Just as I closed my eyes, his arm came around my waist, his hand cupping the curve, and he pulled me to him so that we slept like spoons. Minutes later, as his breathing grew deeper, I heard him mumble, "I love you."

I placed a hand on his. "I love you too."

❄

Christmas Season 2017

"I need Travis this Saturday," I told Jackson early one Monday morning during the first week of December.

He stood at the mahogany Philadelphia highboy, one middle drawer pulled toward him. As he pulled a pair of socks from it, he peered over his shoulder. "For what?"

"To watch Hank. I'm having lunch with Callie and then we're heading to Savannah to do some shopping." I leaned against the doorframe of the master bath, a tube of toothpaste in one hand and my toothbrush in the other. "You do remember that we have a major holiday coming up, don't you?"

He frowned as he shoved the drawer in, not quite reaching its mark of being fully closed.

Jackson rarely fully closed drawers. Subsequently, I'd spent right at two decades of my life going behind him to shut nearly closed drawers.

"I remember," he said. "Paula has already drug out all ornaments and stuff for the local store." Since opening the Savannah location and starting another one in a nearby town, Jackson had taken to calling the Morgan's in Bakersville the local store.

I squeezed a dollop of toothpaste onto the toothbrush. "Thank the good Lord for Paula," I said referring to the bookkeeper who'd been with him since the early days of his running and then owning Morgan's. She'd been a fresh-faced high school senior back then. We'd seen her through a wedding, two kids, a divorce, and another marriage since. She'd gone from thin to shapely to downright stocky, and I loved her to bits.

Jackson sat on the bench at the foot of our bed to don his socks. "Ha. Ha." He slid one foot into a sneaker and said, "Speaking of which, we'll need to go to Steadman's on Sunday so Travis and I can cut down the tree of your choosing."

"After we go to your mom's or before?" I shoved the toothbrush into my mouth, then spoke around it. "Because I'd like to go before." Actually, what I wanted was to go instead of. Sara would be home and I wanted her to go with us before heading back to school.

Jackson frowned again, then bent over to tie both laces. "Go brush your teeth," he said.

I walked to the sink, brushed another minute, spit, rinsed, and then walked back into the bedroom. "I can make an easy lunch here—soup and sandwiches—and then we'll go."

Jackson had made it to the door, one hand on the brass knob, the other clutching his coat. "Okay," he said, then opened the door and walked out.

I followed after him, hurrying on bare feet against a cold floor. "Jackson," I said from the top of the stairs.

He stopped halfway down and peered back up at me.

"Are you leaving already?" I glanced down at the transom window over the front double doors. Darkness still lingered outside, and he hadn't had breakfast yet.

He held up his arm, displaying a watch peeking from beneath a long-sleeved shirt. "Got to. I'm working in two locations today."

I shook my head in disbelief. "Well, did you forget something?"

His eyes closed as he breathed out heavily. He trudged back up the stairs, drew me into his arms, and kissed me. "I'm sorry," he whispered.

"Well," I murmured against his lips. "I *did* brush my teeth."

He patted by backside, which was the first intimate touch he'd given me in two weeks. "Yes, you did." He kissed me once more. "But I really have to go."

"He's hardly home," I complained to Callie that Saturday over burgers and fries. "He leaves before sun up and doesn't get home until after Hank's gone to bed and Trav is nearly ready to crash." I stuck a french fry in my mouth, chewed, and swallowed. "I hardly know what the man looks like anymore."

"Does he know what *you* look like?" she asked, her face flush with that all-knowing look she often gave me.

I reached for another fry. "Meaning?"

"Between work, the kids, the house, and now school—how's that going by the way?"

I nodded, happy for the change in subject. "Really good. I have to complete twenty-six hours on campus at GSU, but I figure I'll do that toward the end. Hank will be a tad older and Travis will be able to drive by then, so . . ."

"So . . . you're hitting the books every night?"

"Every night. Well, except tonight probably. Shopping with you takes some priority."

"When Jackson gets home or before?"

"Usually during. He comes in, and I'm working away." I grinned, so pleased with myself at having taken the steps toward finishing my education. Receiving my diploma. Finally, after all these years. . . .

I picked up another fry.

"So, really, it's not just Jackson. You're both centering in on the things that's the most important to you right now."

I tossed the fry back onto my plate. "Are you blaming *me* for his absence?"

Callie's shoulders straightened. "I'm not blaming anybody, Leesh. I'm just saying."

"Saying what?"

"Saying that you are both working full time, you're both centering in on something you both really want to do, and you have two-point-five children at home, one of which is barely six. It's a lot to take on and still maintain a marriage."

I wanted to hate her at that moment. I wanted to take my entire plate of half-eaten food and throw it at her. But, knowing Callie, she'd pick up the plate and all its contents, set it back on the table, brush off her hands, and say, "There now. Feel better?" And then I'd tell her how sorry I felt about my tantrum and that I knew she was absolutely right. I'd never admit it to Jackson, of course. But Callie, I'd admit any sin to.

"So, you think I shouldn't have gone back to school?" I challenged.

She raised her hands. "I'm not saying that, Leesh. I'm only saying that you two had *both* better pay attention to the most important thing."

"I do pay attention to the kids."

She smiled, but her eyes held what looked to be pity. "I'm not talking about the kids. One of these days, all three of those children will be grown and gone with families of their own. If you and Jackson don't cultivate your marriage constantly, you won't have anything once it's just the two of you."

I reached for my coke and brought the straw near my lips. "Our marriage is *fine,* Callie." I took a sip of my drink before adding, "Can we just go shopping now?"

Callie placed her napkin next to her plate and said, "Grab your coat and let's go," as if nothing ill or strained had been said between us.

We paid our bill and left, then moseyed down the sidewalk toward our parked cars. "Your car or mine?" I asked, hoping she'd say hers. Callie drove a year-old Jaguar with the softest leather interior I'd ever plopped my fanny on.

"Mine," she said with a grin. "I know how you feel about sitting on my leather seats."

I raised my fisted hands and squeezed my face in delight. "It's just *so* wonderfully soft. The leather in my car doesn't compare."

"Nothing compares to a Jag—" Callie stopped, and her eyes focused on something at the end of the sidewalk. "I don't believe it. Is that—?"

I followed her gaze to see a tall silhouette of a fashion statement step out of a shiny new Corvette. "Monica Craig," I breathed out the name. "When did she slither back into town?"

Chapter Twenty-Five

Callie turned to me, eyes smoldering. "Stop that. You know better."

I plastered on a smile, then aimed it at the shapely woman walking toward us in what looked to be a thousand-dollars-if-it-were-a-penny Christmas-red jump suit, arms stretched out for a hug as though we were long lost best buds. "Ohmygoodness," she said in one breath as she reached us. "Callie Everett and Leesha Stewart." She embraced us and we hugged back, me stepping out of the entanglement of arms and the whiff of expensive perfume as quickly as I could without infuriating Callie.

"Callie *Reddick*," Callie said, pointing to herself. "I married Taylor."

Monica waved a hand as if a mosquito had dared invade into her airspace. "I know, I know. Mama told me." She turned to me. "And *you*, Miss Thang. You up and lassoed Jackson Morgan."

Lassoed? I pursed my lips. "Well . . . nineteen years ago."

Monica's head dropped slightly, though not enough to give her swanlike neck a double chin. "I know," she drawled out. "Mama told me."

Callie graciously turned the flow of information back to Monica, whose flawless face I studied for any telltale signs of plastic surgery. "So what about you? We haven't seen you at any of the class reunions or heard of you coming home for a visit."

With a toss of her luxurious mane, Monica declared, "Oh, I know. I know. I've kept Mama in the friendly skies from Atlanta to LA, but—I don't know—since the minute I left here I've stayed so busy. First getting through fashion college—as you know—and then I went right to work in costuming for *The Young and the Restless*—I guess you heard all about that, right?"

"It was in the local paper," I commented.

Monica raised a perfectly tweezed brow. "I'm sure it was, what with the little bit of news that happens around Bakersville. Well, so anyway . . . I finished school, then went right to work, hobnobbed with this one and that one, got married—awful marriage, just awful, but he was loaded to the gills, so I managed to stay with him five disastrous years—and then a nice, profitable divorce later—" She threw her arms up and bent one knee in a classic movie star pose. "—and here I am."

I aimed my attention at her car. "Is that a Black Rose Metallic paint job on that 'vette?"

She looked over her shoulder, then back, her smile widening. "Now how'd you know—oh, that's right. Jackson. That auto parts store thing." She crossed her arms. "How is my old beau, anyway? Still as handsome as ever?"

I thought to claw her eyes out with her own perfectly manicured nails, but before I could strike, Callie answered by saying, "He is as handsome as his wife is pretty."

I smiled in appreciation but Monica's brow shot up again.

"They have three children," Callie continued. "And did you know Taylor and I have twins?"

"Mmhmm," Monica said.

"I'm sure your *mama told you*," I added, then kicked myself for the cat-and-mouse trap I felt myself falling in to.

"Twins?" Monica asked as though she'd just heard the news. "Really?"

"Twelve years old," Callie said. "A boy and a girl. Leesha's youngest is only six."

"And Travis will be thirteen on Christmas Day." I didn't want to get into how old Sara turned on her last birthday, not that I wasn't positive Mrs. Craig hadn't filled Monica in as soon as the news hit nineteen years ago. "Do you have any children, Monica?"

"Oh, gosh, no. No, no, no. Not that I wouldn't *adore* having maybe two . . . or three . . . but I'd rather marry a man who already has them than to have to, you know, go through *all that* to have them myself." She ran her palms over a flat stomach. "I'd never regain this, and I work too hard to keep it."

"Well, you look marvelous," Callie interjected as she wrapped her arm in mine and tugged enough to drop the hint. "We're about to go to Savannah to do a little shopping, so you'll excuse us if we have to hug and run. How long will you be in town for? The month?"

"Oh, honey, no," she said, waving the imaginary mosquito again. "I've moved back."

I halted in whatever step I was about to take. "You have?"

"Don't know if y'all heard, but Mama had a light stroke . . ."

"I'm so sorry," I said, meaning every word of it. "I hadn't heard. Nothing—nothing's been said at church, I don't think." And I could have sworn Mrs. Craig hadn't missed a single Sunday of late. I looked to Callie who shook her head.

"I'm sorry too, Monica," she said. "I hadn't—is she okay?"

Monica blinked several times, and for a crazy moment I wondered if she tried to conjure up tears. "She's fine," she said. "But I felt like . . . you know . . . we just don't know—" Her cobalt blue eyes met mine. "Well, *you* understand, Leesha. One minute they're here and the next they're gone."

An old pain rose up, threatening to choke me. "Yes," I said. "I do know. And I'm sure you made the right decision in coming home." I only hoped she wouldn't make it permanently permanent.

"A man with two . . . maybe three . . . children," I huffed from the passenger's seat of Callie's car.

Callie kept her hands at ten and two on the wheel. "Felicia."

"Seriously, Callie. Have you heard one word about Mrs. Craig having had a stroke?"

She admitted she had not.

"Now you tell me," I continued, "how something like that could go untold in Bakersville."

"I admit, I'm pretty shocked." She pressed a button on her steering wheel. "Hold on." Within a few seconds, Callie's Bluetooth system had dialed a number and brought a Southern "hello" into the car. "Mom," Callie said. "Did you hear anything about Monica Craig's mother having a stroke?"

"A light stroke," I interjected. "Hello, Mrs. Everett," I added.

"Hey, there Felicia," she said in return. "A light stroke? No . . . but Annette Craig and I don't run in the same circles. Still, you'd think we would have heard something, and I haven't noticed her not being in church. Where did y'all hear this?"

"Monica is back in town," Callie said. "Leesha and I just ran into her, and she told us she's moved back because of her mother's stroke."

"Well, I haven't heard tell of it."

"All right then, Mom," Callie said. "Just thought you may know."

"No, hon. I haven't heard a thing."

Callie gave her mother her love then ended the call. "Give Mom ten minutes. She'll have the scoop and will call us right back. Mark my words."

I tucked one foot under the calf of the other leg. "Callie, that Monica Craig is up to something. There's no way a light stroke would have made her come back here."

"I have to agree."

"And can you believe she called Jackson her 'old beau'?"

"That was low. Even for Monica."

"Whatever stink was in her when we were in school has only grown rottener in LA. Trust me. She's up to something."

CHAPTER TWENTY-SIX

Jackson returned home from work that evening at only a few minutes before nine to find me stretched out on the family room sofa in flannel pajamas and fuzzy slippers, watching a Hallmark holiday movie. "Hey," he said. He threw his coat over a chair before plopping on top of it.

I paused the movie and sat up straight. "Hey, yourself. Did you eat?"

He shook his head. "Nah. But I'm not hungry." He gave me his little-boy-hand-in-the-cookie-jar look. "I gotta tell you something."

No, he didn't. I already knew, just by reading his face. "You saw Monica Craig today."

A blush rushed from his cheeks and spread to his ears. "How'd you know?"

"Because *I* saw Monica Craig today."

He straightened. "Did you talk to her?"

"Callie and I did. Uptown. Where did you see her?"

He flinched. "She came by the store."

My whole body tensed. "Did she now . . ." I could imagine what for, and it certainly wasn't 5W-30 motor oil.

Jackson's brow furrowed. "Did she tell you about her mother?"

I nodded. "Mmmhmm. Callie called her mom who knew nothing about it, but then Mrs. Everett called back about fifteen minutes later with 'the scoop,' as Callie called it."

Jackson chuckled as though he were too tired to actually laugh but thankful I hadn't made a scene. "And what is *the scoop*?"

"Mrs. Craig had a stroke but it was only discovered after a routine examination or some kind of test or something. She wasn't even aware of it. If you ask me, Monica is up to something, because her mother is *not* knocking on death's door or even in need of rehab."

"But did you see her car?"

I rolled my eyes. "Men . . ."

My husband's brow wiggled. "She's hot, that much is for sure."

"The car or the woman who owns it?" I challenged.

Jackson paused long enough to make me wonder if he were playing with my emotions or simply thinking over the best way to answer. "Both," he finally said.

I pictured them, then. Jackson and Monica. I couldn't help it. Couldn't stop myself. The two of them, wrapped in each other's arms during that one summer after he and I had decided we couldn't keep our relationship going long distance.

We'd never discussed it, of course. I'd never asked for details about his relationship with her, and he'd never asked me about anyone I may have dated.

But, of course, Jackson *knew* my history. *That* night had been a first for me. He'd known for all our married years that he had been the only man I'd ever been with. Truth be told, he was practically the only boy I'd ever kissed. Not that I'd ever told him in so many words. Let him wonder, I figured.

"Well," I said, hoping my voice held one-part jest and another part serious overtones, "why don't you ditch all this domestic drudgery and run after her. Just think. All *that* and a hot girl too."

"Leesh . . ." He shook his head as though I were crazy for even thinking such a thing, but he blushed again just the same. He looked toward the ceiling. "Where are the boys?"

"Hank is passed out asleep already. Travis ran him ragged today."

Jackson gave the same chuckle he had minutes before. "And Trav?"

I reached for the remote to turn off the television. "Travis Stewart Morgan is on the phone with his first *crush*. We have been asked *not* to interrupt or embarrass him."

Jackson heaved himself out of the chair with a heartier laugh. "Oh, those Morgan boys . . ."

"Don't laugh," I said. "I'm not ready for all this with him."

Jackson stepped over to me and lightly brought my chin up with his fingertips. "Well, you may as well get ready."

I looked up at the man I'd shared the past nineteen years with and all thoughts of him and Monica vanished. We had a solid marriage. We did. Crazy schedules, yes, but we were fine. And we shared three children who were the sun and moon and stars to us both. "It's bad enough worrying about Sara and this Billy person. I can't believe she's not coming home this weekend."

He leaned over and kissed me softly. "Stop worrying," he said. "*They're* fine and *I'm* not going anywhere." His eyes locked with mine. "Not even for a hot . . . car . . . like the one I saw in my parking lot today."

I swatted at him. "Go on," I said, pushing at him with my fuzzy-slippered foot as I stood. "Go shower. I'm exhausted, and we've got church tomorrow."

We headed for the wide doorway leading to the foyer. "Did you get all the shopping done?" he asked.

"Not all. Most." I reached for his hand and he took mine, even as he sighed deeply. "We're still going tomorrow to find the tree, right? You told your mother?"

He nodded. "Yeah. Sara coming home for that, at least?"

"She said she'd try."

"She'll make it. You know how she is about all the traditions surrounding Christmas. Just like her mother."

I squeezed his hand, then released it. "That's the *only* way she's like me."

We walked into our bedroom together, Jackson now halfway out of his shirt. "You're alike in more ways than you realize," he said, yanking it over his shoulders, down his long arms. He clutched it in his hand.

I looked away from him, concentrating on getting the bed ready. Sara being more like me than I realized was what scared me. Could she be easily swayed? Billy was a handsome boy. Tall and well built. Dark, piercing eyes that seemed to read your thoughts. Like Jackson's.

What if Billy said the right words or, having gone through a tragedy, cried the exact right number of tears? What if . . . what if Sara lost her chance at finishing her education? Had to wait, like I had, for nearly two decades?

I shook the fear and worry away. "Go shower," I said again as I reached the bed and tossed throw pillows to the floor.

Jackson stopped at the bathroom door, bare-chested and peering over a muscled shoulder. "Wanna join me?" he asked, his eyes hooded, the familiar blush coloring his face.

I didn't have to think to answer, even though I'd already showered earlier that evening. "Sure," I said.

And then I did.

Monica Craig showed up at church the following morning alongside her mother. She ambled up the center aisle, hugging this one and that one, carrying on as though she were the Queen of England and had recently returned from a tour of the entire British Empire.

"Wow," Jackson breathed out beside me. We stood near "our" row—sixth from the front, right-hand side—talking with Callie and Taylor, waiting for the service to begin.

"Wow, indeed," Taylor added.

I looked at Callie, whose eyes widened as if to say, "Well, she does look amazing."

And she did. I hated to admit it—and I wouldn't in public—but with her hair caught in a loose up-do and her makeup applied just so and her curves caressed by a form-fitting, black wool sheath dress, why wouldn't our husbands stare? I wasn't even sure our pastor would be safe around her.

"I saw that dress on the Neiman Marcus website last week," Callie whispered in my ear.

"What in the world were you doing there?"

My friend grinned at me. "Trolling for all the things I cannot afford."

I looked toward Monica again. "And?"

"One-thousand-twenty-five."

"Is that a *snake*skin clutch?"

"Be good," Callie admonished at the exact moment Monica spied us, squealed with delight, and dashed up the aisle, throwing herself first into Taylor's arms and then into Jackson's.

I held my breath, waiting for her to release him, but once the embrace was over she kept her arm looped in his, smiling up at him, teasing him with her black-lined eyes as she remarked on how "marvelous it had been spending time chatting with him the day before."

Callie shot me a look, but I shook my head.

"Jackson," Monica said, squeezing his arm. "I've been thinking about what you told me yesterday." She eyed me to make certain I followed the conversation.

Jackson had the good sense to appear uncomfortable. "What I—what did I tell you?"

"About the new stores, silly." She turned fully to me. "Can you believe it, Leesha? Our Jackson taking one store and turning it into— what did you tell me, Jackson? Four?"

Four? Before I could open my mouth to correct the number to three, Travis entered the sanctuary from a side door. Jackson, spying the opportunity to disengage himself from Monica, raised his hand. "Trav," he said. "Son?"

Monica breathed out. "Ohmygoodness." She looked at me. "He is the spitting image of Jackson, isn't he? Now what about—didn't you tell me you have a *little* boy?"

"Travis just took him to his classroom."

"And, of course, there's the girl, right?"

The girl. Yes. "She's at Southern," I informed her as the organist took her seat and, with one chord, called the service to order.

"Thank the good Lord," Callie mumbled as we slid into the pew and Monica returned to where her mother typically sat.

But as I sat next to Jackson, I could only hear only one word reverberating through my head.

Four. Jackson had something up his sleeve—something *else* up his sleeve—and he hadn't bothered to share it with me but apparently had managed to talk about it with Monica Craig.

Chapter Twenty-Seven

I threw my purse on our bed and stared my husband, who stood at his highboy removing his watch and the leather bracelet Sara made him while at a church summer camp in her twelfth summer.

"*Four*," I stormed.

Jackson's eyes shot a warning to keep my voice down, so I said it again, this time like the sweet wifey I knew he expected me to be in moments like this, what with our two sons only an earshot away. "Four?"

"You're making something out of nothing." He ripped his dress shirt from the waist of his pants.

I crossed my arms in defiance. "Can you blame me? You tell *me* three and you tell *Monica Craig* four."

Jackson shrugged out of his shirt, then dropped it on the floor. "Why do you do that? Why have you *always* done that?"

I crossed the room to yank the shirt up and march it to the laundry basket in the master bath. When I returned, Jackson had slipped out of his dress pants and was reaching for a pair of jeans. "Do what?"

"Call her *Monica Craig*." He stepped into the jeans. "I don't know a single other person you call by both names. What is it with you and her?" He walked to his closet, jeans still unbuttoned but adjusted around his frame.

"I have *never* liked her, and you know it." I remained planted in front of the bathroom door as though I'd staked a claim.

"Yeah, I know it. I just don't know why." He pulled a sweatshirt from a hanger and then dragged it over his head.

"She's always been so—so—" I couldn't find the right word. "And then that summer you and she—"

He pushed the sleeves of the shirt up halfway to the elbow and then ran a hand over his hair, giving it a tossed devil-may-care look. "What? We dated, Leesh. You and I were done, remember? Or at least we thought we were."

"You and she *dated*, Jackson." Surely he remembered. Surely he'd conjured up memories of her lips against his . . . the way she tasted

. . . the scent of her perfume. And whatever else might come to mind. "Not to mention the way she sidles up to you as if yesterday you'd—like the two of you spent time on that leather sofa in your office—"

Jackson pointed at me. "Now you wait a minute."

I dashed across the room and grabbed his finger. "No, *you* wait a minute. *Four?*"

He jerked his finger from my fist and went to work on the button of his jeans. "Felicia, it was a slip of the tongue. Morris and I have been talking about a second Savannah store. That's all."

"When?"

"Just off and on . . ." He walked toward the door as if the conversation had reached its end.

"No, I mean *when* are you thinking about a second location in Savannah?"

Jackson gripped the doorknob, popped the door open a hair, and then looked back at me. "*After* this third one gets off the ground. The Savannah store is doing good, Leesha, not that you *ever* bother to ask me about it."

"I most assuredly do."

He closed the door and turned fully to me. "When? Name one time you asked."

He had me there. I hadn't asked. As long as he hadn't come in to tell me we had to sell the house and the cars and require Sara to drop out of school, I figured we were all right. But I hadn't *asked* for details. Doing so had never occurred to me. "I'm sorry," I breathed out. "You're right. I haven't asked."

Jackson blinked several times. "Not something I hear every day of the week. An *I'm sorry* and a *you're right* all in the same breath."

He would not make me laugh. I wouldn't allow him so much as a smile. "The point I'm trying to make with you is, you told *her*—"

"The point is," he interrupted, "that it was a slip of the tongue. You gave me an *I'm sorry* so I'll give you one. I shouldn't have spent so much time talking to her, especially knowing how you feel about her. But she caught me unaware."

"She has no boundaries."

He nodded, and his brow came up slightly. A telltale sign if I'd ever seen one. "You're right there." His eyes grew large, realizing what he'd said. "I guess we're even. Two *I'm sorries* and two *you're rights*. Now, can we go downstairs and eat our lunch? I'm hungry, and there's a Christmas tree farm calling our names."

I looked down then up again. "I have to get dressed," I said, throwing my arms up in defeat. "Undressed. Dressed."

Jackson grinned. "I like your second choice the best." Then he walked out the door, closing it behind him.

I breathed a sigh of relief, unaware that the beginning of the end had come.

❄

Christmas Season 2018

Sara and her half-healed heart left to meet Tiffany and Grayson soon after I started dinner, which required throwing everything into a crockpot. Over the past hour, as I'd chopped vegetables, the memories of the previous year had assaulted me, one frame at a time. Monica stepping out of her Corvette uptown. Monica showing up at church. The argument Jackson and I had after we got home.

It had became the first of many, most of which had Monica Craig at the core of it.

I left the warmth of the kitchen, glancing briefly toward the unadorned tree in the living room before climbing the stairs. For some reason, over the past hour, I'd felt the loss of Jackson in a way unlike anything I'd experienced since he'd first left.

In those earlier days—in the heat of summer and constant fighting—I'd been more embarrassed by his departure than heart-sick. Nearly as mortified as I'd been nearly twenty years before when we slipped inexpensive gold bands on each other's left ring fingers and moved into the tiny studio apartment hardly big enough for one, much less two and eventually three. Back then, the shame had both humbled me and made me strong, but now—with Jackson gone and Monica the apparent victor—I sunk under the weight of humiliation. Little by little, I'd grown nearly accustomed to it. To his picking up the kids. Bringing them back. Calling to talk only about the things that concerned them—those three beings who would forever link us.

But in the past hour—perhaps even in the past twelve hours since we'd talked about Sara . . . since he'd admitted that he had been in love with me since high school . . . the hole left by his departure grew large enough for me to fall into.

Was it because he'd confessed the years of his love? He hadn't put a cap on it, after all. He hadn't said, "Since high school until the day I walked out." No. Had he told me last night—had I heard him correctly—that he loved me still?

I entered the bedroom we had shared for so long—the place where we laughed and talked, argued and made up—then stepped from the door to Jackson's old bedroom closet, empty now, except for one item. The one thing he'd left behind—besides his wife and children—but had never returned for. Maybe he hadn't realized it remained. Or perhaps he did. I didn't know. Couldn't know unless I asked. And I dared not ask.

At some point, a single T-shirt had been tossed in the direction of the overstuffed occasional chair in a far corner of the room. After sailing over the back, it landed on the floor, where it remained until after Jackson had been gone for at least a month—maybe six weeks—when in a cleaning frenzy I found it lying wadded up and wrinkled. I brought it to my face, nearly crushed by its sudden appearance, then knelt on the floor, pressed my face into it, and sobbed.

The scent of his cologne and his own masculinity clung to the fibers. I held it as if it were a tiny baby, then rocked back and forth, wishing for all the things that always had been but would never be again. I swore I would never, ever wash it. And I hadn't.

Now, slowly, I opened the closet door and pulled it off the hanger, then crawled onto the bed and buried my face deep within the fabric. Once powerful traces of Jackson had faded in the days and weeks and months. And they would continue to fade. One day, the only bit left would be in my imagination.

Or my memory.

I lowered the shirt to my lap as Callie's words slipped into the room without invitation, demanding my attention. *I didn't ask if he was your husband, Leesha. I asked if you are in love with him.*

"Yes," I whispered into the chilled air without thinking, because the time for trying to decipher was over. "I do. I did. I do." I brought the shirt to my chest and bent over.

Oh, Jackson.

CHAPTER TWENTY-EIGHT

A half hour later I went back down the stairs, made a call across the street, and spoke briefly with Mikey's mom to make sure Hank's being there was okay.

"He's fine," she said. "The boys are eating a snack. I hope that's okay."

"Sure," I said, understanding. The shift of anger to grief had drained me, leaving me with no desire to eat, even as the aroma of the meal simmering in the crockpot lingered throughout the first floor of the house. "Send him home when he gets pesky," I said, inserting a lilt to my voice I didn't feel.

"Oh, then he may never come home," she replied. "He's a wonderful boy."

I thanked her, hung up, and then walked into the family room where I grabbed the remote and turned on the television, flipping through the apps until I found Pandora's Christmas station. Martina McBride's "Hark! The Herald Angels Sing" belted across the room. Too loud if I stayed in the back of the house, but perfect for the living room at the front where I then headed.

Before leaving to meet her friends, Sara begged that the tree be ready for the final decorations by the time she came home. "The least you can do for her," I said out loud with my hands on my hips and my attention on the Fraser fir, "is put the rest of the nineteen ornaments up."

Nineteen. Not twenty, I reminded myself, as there should have been and would have been had Jackson not forgotten our tradition the year before when *other things* kept him preoccupied.

"I've been so preoccupied," he said in his apology on Christmas morning when I reached into my stocking for my annual surprise. "All this going on with the business. I didn't think about it until just now when you—when I—"

"Daddy," Sara gasped, her hand hovering over a large gold bow atop a silver-foiled gift.

"Yeah, Dad," Travis added. "That's like . . . *man*."

Hank popped up from the attention he'd given the deposit Santa had made under the tree in his name. "What?"

I swallowed the hurt. The awkwardness of the moment. Our children were already aware their parents had been fighting more than they'd ever done before. They didn't need this. Not on Christmas Day, of all days. "It's nothing," I said to our youngest. "Just a silly thing—"

But it wasn't silly, and the pain of Jackson's forgetting had become the springboard for everything that followed.

So now here I stood, hands planted on my hips, staring down at the bin holding the remaining ornaments. "Let's get this over with," I said to them as though I expected them to leap out and place themselves on the appropriate branches.

I took my time, displaying each year in such a way as to tell the story of our lives together—because even without Jackson, we were a family. I began at the top of the tree where "Our First Christmas" dangled from one of the short, curved branches, toward the bottom and then circling back to the top where the ornament Jackson had given me to celebrate my advancement at work perched among the needles.

With that mission accomplished, I unwrapped the remaining pieces of the crèche, then placed them on the mantle until—one by one—they found their rightful place among the artificial boughs. Appropriately, an instrumental version of "O Holy Night" began playing from the family room.

I hummed along as I inserted the cord to the tree lights into the wall socket, intent on seeing how the tree looked lit up. Pleased with my achievements, I turned. As I did, Mary's face, shining in the glow of tiny white lights, met mine.

Look at her . . . I'd said to Jackson so many years before.

Leesha. Do we need this?

Oh, Jackson. And look at how sweet the baby Jesus is laying there.

And there's poor Joseph leaning on his staff. Poor man doesn't have a clue what's hit him.

Tears pooled in my eyes. Jackson had spoken from experience. He hadn't a clue what having an unexpected child meant any more than I had.

I looked at Mary again. *And do you think I did,* she seemed to ask. Not that I actually heard her voice. No. But something in her eyes. The innocence. The fear . . .

I stepped closer. From the back of the house, Mannheim Steamroller's "Stille Nacht" played in gentle notes and hums, ushering in a magical moment, even in the middle of the day. Had this been the darkest hours of night—had I gotten up from the depths of slumber and tiptoed downstairs—I would swear I was dreaming. But I wasn't. Outside, the sun closed in on the horizon, the sky was a steel gray, but I was awake, this wasn't a dream, and here I stood with a lovely image of Mary of Nazareth seemingly communicating with me through dark painted-on eyes.

Don't you think I had other plans? What do you imagine I endured to be His mother, this child I had not anticipated so soon? The humiliation? The gossip?

"Let it be as you have said," I spoke aloud, paraphrasing Mary's words to the angel who had brought her the news.

But I was not the Virgin Mother. I had not been impregnated by the Holy Spirit. I had lain my naïve body alongside Jackson's and fallen into a trap offered on a platter of guilt.

But, did it matter? Can you be a little bit pregnant while a little bit unmarried?

No. Mary and I were alike in at least that much. Pregnant and unmarried was still pregnant and unmarried, especially when the rest of the story hadn't been told or understood or lived out.

What was the last thing Jesus said in the Lord's Prayer? Treva had asked. *Look it up,* she'd told me. But I'd overslept the following morning and then . . . I'd forgotten.

It's not Monica Craig, Callie had said. *Come on. You have to figure this out.*

Why don't you just tell me what it is?

You have to figure this out on your own.

I nearly ran up the stairs and into the master bedroom. My Bible and journal rested on the dresser. I cradled the oversized Word in one arm, then crawled onto the bed where Jackson's T-shirt remained. After flipping open the leather cover and thumbing through the pages, I found Matthew's version of the Lord's Prayer.

"Our Father . . ." I read portions aloud. "Your kingdom come . . . daily bread . . . forgive us . . . lead us not . . ."

My right index finger slid along the words until I'd reached the end, the final words, which I read in full. "For if you forgive other people when they sin against you, your heavenly Father will also forgive you. But if you do not"—the text caught in my throat—"If you do not forgive others their sins, your Father will not forgive your sins."

My hand cupped my mouth and I gasped again. I hadn't known. In all these years, I hadn't figured it out or reconciled it. Somehow, I'd thought we were okay because I believed *I* was okay. I had asked God to forgive me, but I had not forgiven myself.

More importantly, I'd never forgiven Jackson. In my heart of hearts, I'd always believed the lion's share of the blame belonged at his feet. He'd been the experienced one. He knew how far was too far. What emotions led to those we cannot turn back from. He should have known better.

In the end, his apology should have been enough. But it hadn't been. I'd dropped a seed of unforgiveness into the fertile ground of our marriage and, over time, I'd watered it and nurtured it until, with the arrival of Monica Craig, the tiny seedling burst from the ground, ready to bloom and produce its poisonous fruit.

"Oh, no," I finally breathed out. "Oh, Jackson. What have I done?"

CHAPTER TWENTY-NINE

A half hour later, I washed my face, applied fresh makeup, then donned the pink sweater Jackson called his favorite along with a pair of slimming jeans and a pair of ankle boots. After an approved look in the mirror, I called Mikey's mom to ask if he could stay a while longer.

"I have to run a quick errand," I said. I stood in the kitchen, my phone tucked between my shoulder and my ear as I dug around in my purse for my keys.

"Not a problem," she said.

I decided I'd call Sara from the car.

When I got in, a look at the dashboard told me I had another twenty minutes before Morgan's locked their front doors. If I got stopped by traffic or a determined red light, I'd have to pull around to the back and hope someone heard me knock on the employee's entrance.

When Sara answered her phone, I told her I had to run up to the store to talk to her father about something.

"You're not going to start something are you?" she asked.

"Not at all."

"Promise me, Mom."

"I promise."

And I wouldn't. Starting something wasn't on the agenda—not that I knew exactly what was. I only knew that what I hoped to do was *end* something. Years of blame. Years of unforgiveness. Years of harboring anger I'd not even known existed until earlier that afternoon.

Five minutes remained before closing time when I pulled into the parking lot. I checked my lipstick in the visor mirror before leaping from the car and hurrying inside.

I should have worn a coat, I thought. The temperature had turned bitter. Or had fear caused a chill? Would Jackson reject my apology? Would we exchange the same cruel words we'd become capable of doling out since a certain someone had returned to town?

I swung open the glass door of the store and hurried in, spying Travis speaking to a customer near a display of floor mats.

"A 2015?" Travis asked, followed by, "Yes, sir." He saw me then, his eyes widening. "Mom?"

I craned my neck. "Where's Dad?"

Travis blushed—assuming the worst, I felt sure. "In his office. Why? Mom?" he called after me, but I was already halfway to the back.

The notion that Monica could be with Jackson struck me then—that perhaps this was why Travis tried to stop me—but I decided not to let the idea or the reality stop me. I'd offer an apology with or without her.

Jackson's door was shut, so I knocked. A second later, I heard, "Come on in," so I opened the door, casing the L-shaped office that, to me, always smelled of tire rubber and Jackson's cologne.

Jackson sat at his desk, alone. He stood when he saw me, his eyes widening, his face flushed much like his son's a moment before. "Leesha . . . what's wrong?"

The door rattled as I closed it behind me. "Jackson." I had to purposely breathe in and out a few times to catch my breath.

He came around the desk, placed his hands on my shoulders and led me to sit on the sofa beneath the observation window whose blinds had been pulled shut. "For heaven's sake, Leesha, what's wrong?" He sat next to me, our knees nearly touching.

I grabbed his hands and he looked down, momentarily stunned into silence.

"I'm sorry," I said, simply and to the point.

Jackson's eyes found mine. "What? What's—"

"I'm sorry," I said again, this time with more force than I'd intended. "I—don't ask me how, but—I had a revelation today." I almost laughed at the absurdity of my declaration. "I know it all sounds crazy, but—I realized—oh, *Jackson*. I've been so angry with you for so long, only I didn't *realize* it until today. I—you and I—we shouldn't have done what we did after your dad died. We know that." I shook my head lightly as Jackson's face registered both surprise and a hint of the old embarrassment. And perhaps frustration at my bringing the subject up for the umpteenth time in our married lives. "But we did. And God—hear me out here—God has been so good to us in spite of our getting things wrong and in spite of me beating that dead horse."

Jackson shared a hint of a smile. We both knew it was true.

"Like you said . . . He uses even the mistakes we make."

"Yes, He does." Jackson's words were so beautifully only a hint above a whisper; they sent warmth through every fiber of my being.

I swallowed hard, both to help myself keep going and to stay focused. "I asked—I asked God to forgive me back then—"

"I know. I did too. Remember? Brother Evan's office?"

Naturally I remembered. I'd wanted to die that day, the two of us, sitting in leather wingback chairs, confessing our sin and our current situation. Asking him to marry us. "But I never forgave me, Jackson," I said, and his brow furrowed. "And I never forgave *you*. You've been nothing but wonderful since the day I told you I was pregnant. You didn't run out on me. You've worked hard, you've provided well, you've been a father your own father would have been proud of, and you've been a wonderful, loving husband. And, all this time . . . in all these years . . . I never . . . " I took a breath.

"Leesha—"

"No. Jackson. Let me finish. I have to finish because this is important." My eyes stayed with his. "I never—never *really*—gave myself to you. I know you think I did, and . . . maybe I thought I had, but I really never did."

Tears welled up in Jackson's eyes, and I squeezed his hands for reassurance. He squeezed back. "Maybe Joseph didn't know what hit him," I said. "But you did, and you didn't run."

"Joseph? Who is Joseph?"

"Never mind," I said, shaking my head. "Jackson, you said something last night."

He scooted closer. Brushed my hair away from my brow with his fingertips. "Did I? What did I say?"

"You said you've been in love with me since high school."

He nodded. "Leesh." He glanced toward the closed blinds. "Gosh, girl."

"Does that mean you're *still* in love with me?" My heart begged him to say yes.

He nodded again as he looked back at me. "You're the most stubborn woman I've ever known, but—yes." His eyes bore into mine.

"Felicia, you're my wife. The mother of my children. That night—when Dad died—you're right. We may have had an error in judgment—no, not we. I take full blame for it—"

"No. That's exactly what I mean, Jackson. This was both of us. I shouldn't have—"

"Stop it. I won't let you do that to yourself. I heard you out, now hear me out."

"All right."

"I realized some time later—probably three months or so into our marriage—that reaching for you was the most natural thing in the world for me to do. Or so it seemed. Almost as if we'd been married our whole lives and always would be."

The words were sweet to hear, but they brought another question to mind. "Jackson," I said, my voice low. "Are you—and please tell me the truth—are you involved with Monica Cra—are you involved with Monica?"

Jackson drew me close, wrapping me in an embrace that nearly squeezed any remaining breath from my lungs, and he laughed. "I promise you. Not now, not ever."

I pulled away to look into his eyes. To see the truth in them. "But in college you two were inti—you know, you were . . . *together*."

He took my face in his hands, stopping me. "Felicia Morgan, you are the *only* woman I've ever been intimate with. My whole life, I swear. Don't you know that?"

"But—" Had I been angry at Jackson for twenty years thinking he'd been the experienced one the night Sara had been conceived? That he should have *known* when to stop? That he should have recognized all the warning signals?

"Monica and I only went out a handful of times. That's it. Whatever designs she had on me were far and above anything I ever felt for her. And I *didn't* feel about her the way I'd always felt about you." He ran his fingertip down the length of my nose. "Look, I decided after we broke up that until I found someone like you, I wouldn't give my heart away." He smiled. "It was always you, Leesh."

The tears I'd held at bay overwhelmed me and the dam burst.

"Oh, Leesha," Jackson said as he shifted back onto the sofa and brought me along with him, holding on for all it was worth. "Is *that* what you thought?"

I nodded and sniffled until Jackson dug around in his back pocket for a handkerchief and held it to my nose. "Blow," he said, and I did.

"I always thought," I said, when I could finally speak, "that first her, then me. But then she was the one who went off to glamourous LA, and I was the one who got pregnant. I was the one who faced the looks your mother gave me and the disappointment of my father and the whole town knew and . . . and . . . then you got to live out your dream while I—"

"What dream?"

I looked around. "This. Morgan's. The stores . . . "

Jackson's eyes softened. "That wasn't my dream, Leesh. I just took what God handed me and made something out of it. Something I hoped Dad would be proud of. My dream would have been . . . I don't know . . . the NFL maybe? Or, at least a shot at it."

Of course. Of course. "I never stopped to realize . . . "

A pause hung in the room, resting between us, no longer pushing against the goads. "Anything else?" he asked. "While we're in up to our necks in all this?"

"I just want you to understand, that's all, that when Monica came back throwing it in my face that she got *her* dream while I got—" I stopped. Looked up at my husband and smiled.

"While you got what? Jipped?"

"*No.* I got the guy. And three amazing children. And a wonderful life I wouldn't trade now for all the diplomas and degrees ever written and rolled up and handed over with a handshake." I sniffled. "It's just that Monica acted like she wanted everything she had *plus* what I had and—"

"She could act all she wanted, Leesha. Give me *some* credit."

I released a pent-up breath. "I have been angry about something that *never* happened. Jealous over a love that never existed."

"Nope. Not for a second."

I looked up at him again. "Can *you* forgive *me*?"

He stared at me for a while before he brought his lips beautifully close to mine. "Consider it done." He chuckled. "I love you, you crazy woman. But I guess you know that."

"I don't think I knew anything at all until today."

His kiss began soft. Sweet. Then it deepened until I pulled away so quickly Jackson seemed taken aback, his face warm with that familiar flush. "What?"

"Oh no you don't," I said with a poke to the chest.

Jackson leaned in for another kiss, his smile wide, his eyes teasing. "Come on. You know you can't resist my charms."

"Yes, I do know," I agreed. "And I also know that every time I fall crazy mad for those charms without—you know—a little careful planning, by some crazy miracle I end up holding a baby nine months later."

He kissed me quickly then, a butterfly lighting on a flower's petal long enough to taste the nectar. "That you do," he said. "That you do."

❄

The wounds of unforgiveness are not healed at once, but by the proper application of time and love. They are also not healed from too far a distance.

Jackson returned home that evening much to the delight of our children, but more to the joy of his wife. We agreed, the two of us, long after the tree had been decorated and the children had laughed themselves silly and then been ordered upstairs, that we'd take everything slowly. That we'd talk more. Work less. And we agreed that we'd give the right amount of time to our children without taking away the necessary amount of time for each other.

Sometime after Jackson and I had gone to bed—after we'd said how much we loved each other and repeated our apologies until we were giddy with laughter over who could say it the greatest number of times—I stretched out next to my husband, my body nestled in the crook of his arm, and my head on his chest as though we had never slept apart a night in our lives. Within a minute, our breathing fell into their familiar rhythm.

Jackson was home. And so was I.

Christmas morning, I woke to find the familiar lump at the base of my stocking and knew that this year—unlike the year before—Jackson had not forgotten the tradition. I dug my hand in, but instead of an ornament box, I drew out a wad of holiday tissue paper tied up by a thin strip of curling ribbon. Holding it up I asked, "What's this?"

Jackson seemed overly pleased with himself. "Open it."

"You don't usually wrap—"

"Just open it, woman," he teased.

I ripped at the paper and, as it fell away, gasped. There, in the palm of my hand, was an exact replica of the first "cookie dough" ornament he'd given me twenty years before. Mr. and Mrs. Mouse. Santa caps on their heads. Lips touching in a tender kiss.

Our First Christmas.

"Oh, Jackson," I said as I held it up, then clasped it near my heart. "How did you ever find this?"

Jackson walked up behind me, then wrapped his arms around my waist. His lips kissed the dip of my jaw beneath my ear and he whispered, "I took a snapshot of the first one and then took it up to Vanessa's. She was able to find it online somewhere. I thought, maybe, it would be perfect hanging near the first, first one," he said and I nodded. "I hope you know," he continued, "that this ornament won't be the last. I'm sticking around long enough to fill that tree with special ornaments, three times around. I'll never leave you again, Felicia Morgan. No matter what." Another kiss, and he added, "You're stuck with me, you know that?"

"For as long as we both shall live?"

"Maybe even after that."

I rested against him. "I can live with that," I said.

He raised a hand then to reveal the most exquisite engagement ring presented between the tip of his thumb and index finger—a large round cut diamond flanked by two trillion cut stones. "And then, many years later . . ." he mumbled.

I turned in his arms. "Oh, Jackson," I said again. "You didn't need to—"

He cut off my words with a kiss that left the children sputtering.

"Get. A. Room," Travis moaned.

"Hush-up, Trav," Sara admonished.

"Why would they need a room?" Hank asked, his voice rising in innocence. "They've *got* a room."

Jackson and I collapsed in laughter. "Why, yes, son," Jackson said. "I believe we do."

I held my left ring finger up for him to slip the ring on. "It fits perfectly," I said as though I were Cinderella donning her glass slipper.

He kissed me again, then spoke against my lips. "I wouldn't have it any other way."

I slid my arms around his neck, my toes straining to meet his height as my gaze slid over his shoulder to the mantle. To the crèche where Mary knelt over her swaddled babe—the one I'd placed in the manger the evening before. She'd not expected such a thing in her life—such a miracle. Yet, there she was—or an artist's impression of her—adoring Him with praying hands and a wistful smile.

Then, for a moment, I imagined that her contemplation left Him long enough to find me, blissful in my husband's arms. And, for a moment, I imagined that she smiled.

Acknowledgments

It's not unusual to read a quote by a famous writer (or to see a meme out there in social media) expressing the loneliness associated with the art of writing. We, those of us who write for a living, are often visualized by adoring fans as sitting tucked away somewhere, completely cloistered, scribbling away in notebooks or tap tapping on a keyboard. While that may be true from time to time, writing is not as solitary as it is believed. Even alone, the muse shows up . . . and the writer is no longer alone.

And so it is with my work and, in particular, this work. Allow me, then, to thank a few folks who have been a part of creating *The Ornament Keeper*.

Thank you, Jonathan Clements, believing agent. You continue to have a faith in me I'm not sure even I possess some days. Thank you to Ramona Richards and the entire New Hope Publishers team for believing in this work.

Word Weavers International's Page 6—my peeps! My first readers, you're amazing (Oh, Bruce Brady, that you could see this completed.). Cynthia Howerter, my critique partner, that you woke early in the mornings with this on your mind, searching for ways to improve, means so much to me.

A huge thank you to my beta readers (and I hope I remember everyone): Donna Postell, Deanne Henry Field, Marilyn Stump, Willene Keel, and Deana Dick.

Thank you to my family, especially Dennis Everson, who doesn't mind when I take a month or so, lock myself in my office, and rarely come out because the words won't stop coming. You are the one who recognizes that faraway look I often get . . . and actually appreciates that I can be in a room . . . and yet *not* . . .

Thank You, sweet Lord. You are the Giver of the talent. You are the door opener. You are the one who showed me that little verse of Scripture so many of us often miss (or ignore). Thank You for the month of July . . . when life slowed down enough to usher in the story of Jackson and Leesha.

Finally, thank you, kind reader. I hope *The Ornament Keeper* was everything you wanted (or needed) it to be.

Eva Marie Everson
March 2018

If you enjoyed this book, will you consider sharing the message with others?

Let us know your thoughts at info@newhopepublishers.com. You can also let the author know by visiting or sharing a photo of the cover on our social media pages or leaving a review at a retailer's site. All of it helps us get the message out! Twitter.com/NewHopeBooks Facebook.com/NewHopePublishers Instagram.com/NewHopePublishers

---

New Hope® Publishers is an imprint of Iron Stream Media, which derives its name from Proverbs 27:17, "As iron sharpens iron, so one person sharpens another."

For more information on ISM and New HopePublishers, please visit IronStreamMedia.com NewHopePublishers.com

This sharpening describes the process of discipleship, one to another. With this in mind, Iron Stream Media provides a variety of solutions for churches, missionaries, and nonprofits ranging from in-depth Bible study curriculum and Christian book publishing to custom publishing and consultative services. Through the popular Life Bible Study and Student Life Bible Study brands, ISM provides web-based full-year and short-term Bible study teaching plans as well as printed devotionals, Bibles, and discipleship curriculum.

OTHER CHRISTMAS FICTION FROM
NEW HOPE

~~$15.99~~ **$3.99**

~~$15.99~~ **$3.99**

~~$15.99~~ **$3.99**

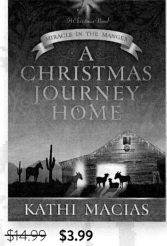

~~$14.99~~ **$3.99**

VISIT **NEWHOPEPUBLISHERS.COM**
FOR MORE INFORMATION.